WILD HUNT

a vampire novella

by

NANCY KILPATRICK

Baskerville Books

This book is a work of fiction. Names, characters, places, businesses, and incidents either are the products of the author's imagination or are used in a fictitious manner. Any similarity to events or locales or persons, living or dead, or undead, is entirely coincidental.

No part of this publication may be reproduced, stored or transmitted, in any form, or by any means whatsoever (electronic, mechanical, etc.) without the prior written permission and consent of the author.

First Edition 2019
Copyright © 2019 Nancy Kilpatrick
Cover Design: Istvan Kadar
Cover research: Sue Dent
Interior Design: Cheryl Freedman
All rights reserved
ISBN: 978-0-9813249-2-0

Acknowledgements

My thanks to Heather Taylor and Sam Reeves for their editing expertise, and to Sarah Burrows, Diana Price and Janet Rahn for proofing skills. I couldn't have written this story without foreign language translations and I'm grateful to Istvan Kadar (Romanian), Kevin Nunn (Irish), and Uwe Sommerlad (German). Also, my thanks to C. Soles for the background image and print book formatting, Cheryl Freedman for work on the print book, Istvan Kadar for the lovely book cover design, various knowledgable folks helping with all sorts of other madness including JNMoon, Jason Graves, Michaelbrent Collings; Heide Goody, Sam Reeves, Eric Kauppinen, Rick Chiantaretto, et al, and my deepest gratitude to Sue Dent for her massive amount of research work on early cover designs and her kindness and generosity in answering my endless tech questions along the way in a variety of capacities. I'm also grateful to David Dodd for walking me through the ebook manuscript upload. Everyone knows I'm a tech idiot! And I am extremely grateful to Baskerville Books for their work resulting in *Wild Hunt* finding a home.

I also want to express a special appreciation to you who are readers and vampire fans. There are a LOT of vampire fans out there. Despite what anyone may tell you to the contrary, you are no longer weird!

Praise for Wild Hunt

"Nancy Kilpatrick writes with intelligence and depth, her stories both innovative and captivating. She writes short stories masterfully, giving you everything you need to be thoroughly entertained within just a few pages. What I find most impressive in her tales is how brilliant and emotionally driven they are."

Moonlight (aka Amanda), reviewer - *Vampires*

✟

"I enjoyed every drop. "Wild Hunt" is a stand-out tale. Honestly, I would pay much more than I did for that story."

Lydia Peever, reviewer - *PostScripts,* nightface.ca

✟

"Kilpatrick makes vampires fun, scary and interesting again."

Michael D. Griffiths, reviewer - *SFReader.com*

✟

"Vampires from Nancy Kilpatrick's imagination become some of the most wickedly unique I have ever read."

Sam Reeves reviewer - *samreevesblog.blogspot.com*

✢

Table of Contents

✢

Acknowledgements

Praise for Wild Hunt

A Definition

Dear Reader

Wild Hunt

Dear Reader, Thank You!

Excerpt from *Revenge of the Vampir King*

About the Author

A Definition

A **Wild Hunt** (*Wilde Jagd* in German) is a folklore motif wherein supernatural hunters carry out vengeful acts. Any female who gets in their way is in grave danger of being abducted—or killed!

Dear Reader

Wild Hunt is a vampire story where you can choose *your* preferred happy ending. If you're satisfied when you reach the three ☥☥☥ then stop there.

However, 3 is the number of change. You might just want to keep reading to the end of the novella!

Nancy Kilpatrick

WILD HUNT

As Lorelei lifted the nylon flap, searing heat whooshed into the tent accompanied by ear-splitting instrumentals. The temperature was exceptional for the end of May. Earlier in the evening she'd overheard people commenting about global warming. And someone speculated that the gates of Hades must be wide open.

A mass of human bodies jumped and swayed and swung their arms to the sounds blasting from the giant speakers on the stage, but she could not see them clearly; the stage rear faced her and the night was dark. The music, though, stirred her soul. She listened as the bass guitar and keyboard dialogued, accompanied by poetic vocals that swirled through the notes and slid deep inside her.

The fans who had come to this year's Wave-Gotik-Treffen festival in Leipzig were hell-bent on draining the last drops of musical excitement from the air. The annual festival was winding down and the Sisters of Mercy, or at least Andrew Eldritch, had agreed to play one more song, making the crowd of alternative music freaks scream and yell in utter abandon.

Eldritch had come by for a Tarot reading earlier in the week, but then so had many of the musicians playing at the festival. They all asked the same questions; most wanted fame and fortune in some measure although queries were usually disguised with the words *art* and *creativity*. Every last one of them had insisted on the cards rather than the ball, just so they'd have something visual to focus on and talk about later. Lorelei didn't mind, although she believed Tarot wasn't as exact as the crystal, at least for her readings.

She dropped the flap and returned to the tent, taking the small steps she had become used to ever since her vision had gone wonky ten years ago, the day she turned eight.

She'd been playing in her parents' backyard and, for no reason that made sense to her now, looked up at the sun during a solar eclipse. Something in that brilliance reminded her of her grandmother, as if the old woman was in the sun, waving at her: hello or goodbye. When she stopped staring at the sun, her vision was hazy and had been that way ever since.

Several eye specialists diagnosed corneal flash burn that spread from the center of the cornea almost to the edges, much like the sun eclipsed by the moon. It might clear up, with time, they said. But it hadn't yet. All she was certain of was that since then, visually, nothing had been clear. On a good day with decent lighting, she could see with some clarity through a thin circumference ring that surrounded the haziness.

She'd gotten over being bitter and had come to the conclusion that at least she wasn't totally blind, and that had to mean something. Most important, she could read cards, but especially the crystal ball. For some reason, the haziness let images form in her mind when she searched the crystal for answers, answers that usually proved startlingly accurate.

Just before her mom died, the same year as her grandmother, one day, out of the blue she said: "Daughter, you've inherited an extraordinary gift. More than your grandmother's ball, you also have her prescience; you can read the crystal. You can see the future."

She passed the reading table which was in the center of the space so that she could easily navigate around it and moved to the back of the tent. She felt under the cot she slept on that one of the festival's organizers had put in the tent for her to use. Her fingertips contacted the large rolling suitcase. Lorelei slid her hand along the hard plastic to the handle and pulled it out.

Once she'd placed the suitcase onto the cot and opened it, she reached under the narrow bed again and found the milk crate with her clothes and began scooping them out of the crate and into the suitcase. She hadn't brought much, since she was only here for a week. Three outfits besides what she was wearing, an extra pair of shoes, daily underwear, and the corset she had on today over the black lacy blouse and ankle-length ebony silk skirt with the zipper in the back. By feel, she pulled out the simple, stretchy black dress she usually stored in the shoulder bag she carried, just in case.

Besides the silver *Alchemy* necklace of a vampire bat she was wearing, and a copper Steampunk ring from *Catherinette*, she'd brought along an antique rosary that had also been her grandmother's, a sterling rat earring for good luck she'd ordered from XtraX, an earring made of surgical sutures, an extra nose ring, two more ear cuffs, and a bracelet composed of twisty PVC shaped like barbed wire that had been her mom's when she was young. Most of the jewelry was already in a small pouch that she stuffed into an inner pocket of the suitcase.

Another plastic crate held toiletries and the little bit of makeup she wore, mainly face powder and a touch of dark lip gloss. Her dad said she'd been blessed with her mother's copper-red hair and eyebrows and his hazel eyes veering towards green. He assured her that her lashes were wispy and long enough that she didn't need makeup. It was just as well, since she couldn't really see clearly enough to apply it.

She found the extra boots she'd brought—the eighteen-hole Doc Martens—and slipped them into a plastic bag from the inside pocket of the suitcase, closed the case and pulled it off the cot and onto the packed-dirt floor.

Next, she tightly rolled up the sleeping bag on the cot and attached it to the suitcase with a bungee cord. All she needed to do was wrap the cards in the red-velvet fabric and pack them, the ball and the dress in her shoulder bag and she could be on her way before the massive retreat.

This was her third year at the festival—three was the number of change—and she knew from experience that while some people liked to linger, not wanting the event to end, most were eager to get an early start back to where they came from. Those that stayed around were usually too drunk or high to want readings. She'd learned to try to get ahead of the pack.

She hadn't brought that much food, and pretty well everything she had hauled from home had been eaten except for a couple of apples. At least the Styrofoam cooler was empty, which she'd leave behind—one less thing she had to cart out of here.

She would have to find a ride to Frankfurt, then she could call a friend to pick her up. Usually there were plenty of people feeling good from the weekend and she had never had problems getting a lift in or out of the festival and last year got a ride right to her door and...

Suddenly, she felt a chill run up her spine. Still holding the two apples, she jolted upright. Now, behind, she briefly heard the sound of the crowd rise in volume and then die, and with it, the hairs at the nape of her neck rose. Someone had opened and closed the tent flap. Lorelei turned around and her eyes and the dim candlelight let her see only a vague form standing just at the tent entrance who looked like a shadow, or a dark ghost.

"*Geschlossen*," she said. She'd been born in Germany to a German father and Irish mother so she could speak two languages and most of her clients spoke German or English. She'd also picked up a smattering of several other languages, as did most Europeans.

When she didn't get a response, she repeated what she'd said in French, Spanish and then finally said in English, "I'm closed."

The guy—and she could sense it was a guy—stood perfectly still. She had a vague image of long dark hair, black clothing, some metal glinting in the candlelight that might be chains hanging from parts of his outfit. In other words, he was dressed like most of the males here.

"I want answers," he said in English, which wasn't his first language. Her ear over the last week had attuned to many new accents but his wasn't one of them.

It had been a long week and she was tired. But something about him just standing there told her that he was determined to get answers and the quickest way around this would be to give him a reading and hope that the spiritual world would provide what he needed.

She didn't think he was a druggie—he didn't emit the scent. In fact, he didn't have *any* smell. Her senses other than sight were sharp, mainly because she'd made an effort to develop them, and that included the sixth sense, ESP.

"Alright," she said, placing the apples on the cot, and then moving her normal path towards the table. She took a seat on her chair, which faced the entrance. "Please," she said, "come in," gesturing to the chair opposite hers.

He hesitated but eventually moved into the tent and sat down.

This close, she could see him better, although, of course, she still couldn't make out details, just that his eyes seemed as dark as his hair, his skin pale by contrast. He might be good looking, she didn't know. Looks weren't at the top of her list of preferable traits anyway, since they don't matter if you can't see them.

"I charge ten euros for a reading. I read cards, which most people prefer. I also read the crystal," she said, nodding her head towards the large ball on the table between them. "Which would you like?"

"I don't care." He sounded angry.

"Then I'll choose for you," she said quickly, and decided on the ball.

"Put your hands here." She indicated that he should grip the ball on each side. When he didn't move, she added, "It's okay. It's safe. It won't hurt you."

"It can't hurt me," he snapped. "I want answers."

"I'll give you answers, but you have to participate. I can't do it alone." She could, of course, but this would be more accurate, and something told her she needed to be accurate for this reading.

Finally, reluctantly, he put his hands on the ball and she placed hers gently over his. And nearly pulled away. It was like touching a block of ice! His hands were freezing! It was at least thirty Celsius outside and probably twenty-eight inside the tent, and none of that explained this!

"Your hands are cold," she said, hoping for an explanation.

"I am always cold," he told her, which wasn't an explanation at all.

Lorelei did not pursue it. She'd already felt the vibe of weirdness coming off him even before he sat down, and it was starting to unnerve her so she decided to just do the reading and get it over with. Then she could get out of here and go home.

Finally, she gazed down into the ball.

At first she saw nothing, but that was normal. Many times, the crystal hid its secrets and she just had to be patient until it was ready to reveal something. But, finally, an image did form, swirling like a mist, and she let it speak through her. "You are the youngest of three boys. Your mother's favorite, but not your father's."

She felt one of his finger's twitch.

"One of your brothers...there are only two of you left. You and your oldest brother. You don't get along. He's a corporate type, you're artistic, intuitive, emotional, creative, sensitive..." She felt his fingers tense as he gripped the ball tighter.

The swirling within the crystal picked up speed and she wondered about that. Normally, images slowed down. Why this sped up she didn't know but waited until something else formed that she could identify and then she said, "You have a problem. A big problem. You're searching for something, or, more, someone. I see a lot of loss, pain and anguish and—"

Suddenly he leapt up, breaking contact with her, with the ball. His chair and the table fell over. The ball thudded onto the dirt. Before Lorelei could get to her feet, his cold hand grabbed her by the throat. He lifted her off the chair and then rapidly shoved her backwards across the room until she crashed up against the back of the tent, braced by the tree that stood just behind that canvas wall.

Lorelei pulled at his hand with both of hers, struggling to pry away his steely fingers. Her breath was cut off and she fought for air, not able to get any into her lungs.

"Where is he?" came a voice as cold as the flesh.

She tried to speak but couldn't and he must have realized that and loosened his grip enough that she could gasp in a few breaths. Finally, she choked, "Who? What are you talking about?"

"Don't act stupid! You know!"

"Please, I don't—"

Suddenly, he threw her sideways and she fell onto the cot. He was on her in a second, ripping the high lace collar of her Victorian-style blouse, exposing her throat. Now he had a smell, an overwhelming odor, coppery, sharp. She couldn't be totally sure of what this was because it didn't make sense, but understood completely the instant his sharp teeth found her neck.

And then, in a blindingly-fractured second, he yelled as if he was being burned alive. His body repelled away from hers, shoved back hard by an invisible force. When he stopped, he took several steps further back and then stood perfectly still.

"What are you?" he hissed in a low voice.

Lorelei took a moment to get her breathing under control and to try to calm her body's trembling. She waited until her heart's rapid pounding slowed a bit and then sat up. She felt her neck, but there was nothing wet, no blood; he hadn't pierced the skin. Of course he hadn't!

All the while he stood rooted to the spot and she sensed him watching her.

Finally, she stood. On shaky legs, she edged past him to the table, which she managed to right, and her chair. The ball had rolled only a short distance and had stopped not too far from the table leg. Heavy crystal, it wouldn't break easily, although it might have chipped again. That had happened before, not too long ago. She picked it up and felt all around, finding the first chip and now a second and she sighed.

The holder was more difficult to locate and she had to get on hands and knees and pat the ground for it but finally her fingertips touched the concave plastic. She picked it up and put it onto the table then carefully perched the ball on the rim of the cup-like holder.

She sat down and stared into the crystal. The swirling image was as she had last experienced it, but now it slowed and she was able to read what it was trying to tell her. Still staring into the ball she said absently, "Vampire, you can't have my blood, but you can have answers, if you still want them. Sit down."

She heard a low sound behind her, something between a hiss and a growl. It unnerved her, but she had experienced the worst. He couldn't really harm her, at least she didn't think so, if what her grandmother had told her was accurate, and so far it seemed to be.

He was prideful. Unaccustomed to taking orders, or even suggestions. She didn't need the crystal to tell her that. But the swirling did mention that he was a prince in a long line of night creatures. Royalty, she thought. Dark, undead royalty. In need of answers. And he can only get them from a peasant like me! She smiled. It was going to be a long night.

"Alright, *nosferatu*, let's start over. You need to put your hands on the crystal so it will pick up your energy."

"You are blind!" he snapped, stating the obvious like an accusation.

"Partially blind. I can see the images, the messages."

She waited patiently. Finally, he righted his chair and sat. He took a rebellious moment before placing his hands on the clear round stone.

Lorelei placed her warm hands over his cold ones as before and stared into the ball.

"How do you see if you cannot see?" he demanded, again in that disapproving tone that said he didn't trust her. She almost laughed. Almost. *He* didn't trust *her*! Ha! She didn't bother answering, since he wouldn't understand, even if she could convey it.

The swirling inside the crystal formed an image that was pretty clear and would have been to anyone. "You're on a vendetta," she said. "You're searching for someone, a relative. Maybe it's your brother or father, but maybe someone else, like an uncle. It's a male and someone close in blood. This isn't your fight, though. You've been sent on a mission and you're obligated to find him and..." She paused, then said delicately, "...do away with him."

She looked up at his face. Still, she could not discern features, but something there had shifted, maybe his energy.

"Where will I find him?" he asked, his tone less harsh than before. She picked up an undertone: fear? remorse? confusion? He was hiding from her so it was hard to tell.

"I don't know."

His hands turned quickly and he grabbed her wrists. "You do know! He was here five nights ago, a week at most. Where is he now?"

His chilly hands felt like glacial handcuffs, hard, permanent, freezing her flesh. "I don't know what—"

"Tell me!" he demanded.

He turned both wrists and she cried out in pain, "Don't hurt me! I don't know. I can help you find him, but not like this."

He flung her wrists away from him. "What are you?" he asked again. "Why is there a barrier between your blood and me?"

She rubbed her wrists and stared away from him. "You wouldn't believe me if I told you and I can't tell you anyway. I only know the myths and legends and they are true. It's how I know what you are. How your teeth could not enter my vein. I know what you are because my grandmother told me you would come and what would happen. And I know that I can help you find the one you're looking for but not here, not now. I have to travel with you."

"No!" he said sternly.

"Then you'll never find him."

He leapt up from the table and grabbed her upper arms, lifting her to her feet. "You will tell me!"

"I can't! I can't see that far into the future for a precise question like this. Not from here. I have to go with you and read the ball along the way. If you want to find him, I have to go with you."

Obviously he was staring, his face inches from hers, his cold coppery breath on her cheek, the chill from his hands penetrating the flesh of her lace-covered arms.

He shoved her away and she fell onto the dirt, landing on her butt. He turned and stomped towards the tent flap.

"You won't find him on your own," she warned. "There's some sort of spell on him, or some invisible cloaking he's capable of, I don't know. You need someone like me to see through it."

He stopped just at the flap. She waited, knowing he was sifting through all the alternatives, coming to the only possible conclusion. He turned slowly.

Lorelei got to her feet.

His voice became deeper as he said, "*Vei plati pentru nesupunerea, vrajitoarea!*"

When she didn't respond, he said, "You speak a little of a few languages but do you understand mine?"

"No," she said. "Is it Romanian?"

"Yes."

"You're from Transylvania. I saw that in the ball. Are you a descendant of Vlad Țepeș?"

"Very good. You are learning." His tone was condescending.

"And will you translate what you said?"

"You will know soon enough, *vrajitoarea!*"

"In your language, you are *vampir*."

"Yes."

"Then you called me a witch. And probably threatened me with bodily harm."

He didn't answer, but she knew she was right. Not because she had guessed that the word *vrajitoarea* meant witch, but from the way he spoke, she grasped the fuller meaning. Besides, she'd heard that word before. Recently. The other vampire from Romania, the one he was hunting. He had used it, and a translation.

"Yes, you are learning. And I will teach you. To obey me."

She didn't know what to say to that, or to anything else. If her grandmother hadn't foretold these events and conveyed them to Lorelei, she would have been terrified and have already died of fright at coming into close contact with a vampire, no, *two* vampires in the same week. But it was her destiny. One she had prepared for all her life. And now, she knew, she had to go with him. She had to see this to the end.

She gathered the crystal ball in her arms, picked up the holder and the cards and the cloth and turned her back on him as she walked to the cot. She wrapped the cards in the velvet and stuffed everything into the thick leather bag leaning against the suitcase handle that she kept with her at all times, which already held a travel-size toothbrush and paste and an extra pair of underwear. She felt along the cot for the black dress and shoved that in too. Her hands roamed over the cot surface until she located the apples. One had been squashed when he jumped her.

The other seemed in good enough shape. She tossed it into her shoulder bag for later and slung the wide strap of the weighty sac across her chest, then felt for the suitcase, raised the handle and dragged it behind her.

"Lead on, Lord of the Night."

"You mock me at your peril," he snapped.

"I think peril is probably what this is all about, so don't take it personally."

He turned and left the tent, dropping the flap so she'd have to lift it herself. After all, she thought, he's royalty. He doesn't do anything for anyone. Well, we'll see how far that gets him.

☦

He led her through the grounds, music blasting from various directions. It was later than Lorelei had wanted to leave here and the crowds were no longer occupied by performances on the main stage. She had to struggle to get through the throngs.

Several people who had come for readings recognized her and wished her *Gute Reise!*, *Bon voyage!*, Good trip! and two offered her a ride, which she declined. She sent the warmth back, knowing it was likely the only warmth—not to mention human contact—she would have for a while.

The night was still humid and she began to sweat from the effort of lugging the suitcase and the heavy shoulder bag at a pace she would not normally walk, struggling to keep up with him. Darkness took most of the remnants of vision she possessed and obliterated them. She had no idea where the vampire was, or if he was still there. She moved by instinct alone, and eventually she reached a large parking lot.

Many people were loading vehicles and at least there were headlights so she could make out vague forms and stop walking into everyone. Still, she was jostled by the crowd.

She paused where she was, not knowing which way to go. Suddenly she felt an icy touch as fingers encircled her upper arm. He led her through the throng as she pulled her suitcase along, accidently bashing it into people with an "*Entschuldigung!*" and "Sorry!"—she had no sense of direction and had lost perspective on the larger number of bodies surrounding her and their proximity to her own.

Finally he stopped. She heard a triple beep as the vehicle doors were remotely unlocked. What she could see in this dim light of only headlights was a very large dark car, more like an American-made truck or a van. He opened the back and said, "Put inside your valise."

Pulling it had been one thing, lifting the full case another, especially with the weight of the shoulder bag on her petite body, and she struggled with it until finally he deigned to help her. He took the suitcase in one hand and lifted it up easily, like it weighed nothing, then closed the back door and gripped her arm as if she might try to run away.

Standing next to him now, she had a better sense of height—he had about five or six inches on her, but then most people were taller than five foot four.

He opened the front passenger door and said, "Go in."

She felt the seat back and the height of the seat itself. The vehicle was very high and she had to feel around further to determine where to step up so she wouldn't fall and what she could hold onto.

She must have taken too long in her assessment because suddenly he turned her to face him and lifted her by the waist, placing her onto the seat as if she was a child. He was so impatient that he didn't wait for her to turn her feet but lifted them and placed them onto the floorboard, then slammed the door.

Seconds later he was in the driver's seat starting the engine.

She felt behind her on the right and the left, searching for the seatbelt. "You do not need it," he said. "You will not be dying in a traffic accident, although I can offer no guarantee against another cause of death."

"Thanks for reassuring me. I'd prefer wearing a seatbelt on the *autobahn*."

He reached across her and pulled the belt down from her right, over her body, and then snapped it into the clip.

"Thanks," she said, wondering why she bothered.

He maneuvered the vehicle out of the crowded parking lot and took the narrow road to the highway at as fast a clip as the number of vehicles on the road allowed. As she expected, the *autobahn* was bumper to bumper. He drove only to the next exit and then they left the highway behind.

After about half an hour, or so she guesstimated, she said, "Where are we going?"

He didn't answer.

She pulled out her cell phone and he said, "Do not make any calls!"

"I'm not." She pulled the ear buds from her bag and held them up. "Just listening to music." But once she had the buds in, instead of music she pressed by feel and by count the cover of an audio book three down from the top, one she was very familiar with, and when it started she pressed the buttons she was also familiar with then scrolled to the spot she wanted, again, by counting the number of finger swipes.

She listened for quite a while, maybe another half hour, and finally took the buds out of her ears and said to him, "If you want to find your relative, I have to read the crystal. We might be headed in the wrong direction."

When he didn't respond, she lifted the buds to replace them, saying, "As you like," but stopped when he shot back,

"Always, *vrajitoarea*."

"I'm not a witch, you know," she said. "I just have a few psychic abilities, like my grandmother."

"In Romania, this is how we call your kind."

"That's a bit old-fashioned, don't you think?"

"Fashion does not alter over the centuries as much as you would imagine," he said, and she was surprised he was being so talkative all of a sudden. She took advantage of it, curious about the things she couldn't see.

"So, how old do you look, I mean, in human years?"

"I resemble a man thirty-five to forty years. The age at which I accepted my heritage."

He looked the same age as her dad! How strange was that?

"But you've been alive, or undead—if that's the right term—longer, right?"

"I have existed for more than three centuries."

"Really? So you're almost a direct descendant of Vlad Țepeș, a few generations removed."

"He was my great great great granduncle. My father is the son of his brother's son's son's son."

"Uh, right." She thought for a second then said, "Vlad had two half-brothers, Mircea II and Vlad Călugărul, and he also had a younger brother, Radu cel Frumos—Radu the Handsome he was called, if I remember correctly."

He turned to look at her. "You know much about my lineage."

"Everyone knows this. Well, everyone who's into vampires, which is a lot of people nowadays.

"Anyway, Mircea II was buried alive. That's something you don't forget. Radu the Handsome, well, after he and Vlad III were imprisoned by the Ottomans as children, he converted to Islam. He was kind of a monkish sort anyway, so maybe he had children, but maybe not. I don't think you're descended from either of them.

"Now, Mircea and Vlad Dracula, that's another story. Mircea's name was also Vlad—he was II and Vlad Dracula was III, so I'll just call them two and three, if you don't mind—no disrespect intended. From what you tell me, you're likely descended from two—Mircea—and I suspect the other vampire you're searching for is in the same line. Am I right?"

"Is this book knowledge, or did you see it in the clear rock?"

"Neither. I heard most of it on my phone just now, on an audiobook on vampires I'd downloaded. The rest, the other vampire told me."

He hit the brake so hard she was glad she was wearing the seatbelt. "You told me you did not know him!"

"I didn't say that. I said I didn't know *where* he is. Of course I met him. I didn't know it was him until you tried to bite me, then, when I realized you're undead, I knew it was the other undead you were searching for. He tried to bite me too, with the same result. I read his future."

"And what is his future?"

She turned and stared in his direction and sensed he was staring back at her. "His future involves a fight with another like him. The crystal wasn't clear about who he would fight but now I'm guessing that would be you."

"And which of us will win this battle?"

"I couldn't say. Like I told you, I need to be closer for such a specific question. That's why I'm here, right."

"Why are you not with him?"

"Because I'm supposed to be with you."

He paused a long time before the vehicle moved again. The sky was black as ink and the road they traveled had no other cars. She knew she should feel intimidated but held onto the fact that he couldn't take her blood. And he needed her, even if he wasn't wholly convinced of that.

Lorelei had seen more of the future of the other vampire than she admitted to. It wasn't her job to interrupt destiny but to be the conduit through which it actualized. That she would be part of that actualization filled her with dread, but she wouldn't give in to fear. Her grandmother had predicted all this, and Lorelei knew this was her own destiny and destiny would be fulfilled, one way or the other.

He pulled off the road onto a narrower road, a wide dirt path really, from the bumpy ride. Tree branches swiped the vehicle on both sides with hard thwacks as he drove too quickly. They traveled for about one minute when he came to a stop. She figured it was too dark to see where they were, even if she'd had vision at her disposal.

He opened his door and got out, then she heard the rear door open and had the sense he was moving her suitcase. Suddenly her door opened.

"Come out," he said.

She fumbled with the seatbelt but couldn't figure out how this one worked. Finally he shoved her hands away impatiently and unsnapped the belt. She turned in the seat and gripped the door frame on both sides and gingerly moved her feet, trying to discern where to place them so she could get some purchase because the vehicle was high and she was afraid she would have to jump down.

"How do you get around?" he snapped, gripping her waist, lifting her to the ground. She knew it was a rhetorical question and didn't bother to answer.

He had a firm grasp on her upper arm and walked her to the back of the vehicle. She realized that no branches were hitting her so they must be in a clearing.

"I need to use the bathroom," she said.

He sighed heavily and told her, "Go into the bush."

Without light, she was totally blind. She put her hands out in front of her, feeling only air. "Which way?"

He turned her and said, "Ahead, five or six paces."

She moved forward, her arms out in front like a ghost, the heavy shoulder bag weighing her down. Soon she felt the bark of a tree and the branches extended from it higher up. This was a wide tree, probably an oak from the distinctive scent, and she felt her way around it to what must be the other side. Briars snagged her silk skirt en route and she knew it would be ruined.

Finally, when she felt she was safe from his view, she lifted her skirt, pulled down her underwear and squatted, listening to the sound as she relieved herself—it was the only sound, which now struck her as very strange. No night creatures scurrying in the underbrush, no hooty owls, no swish of leaves swaying in the warm and slight breeze.

She located a couple of tissues in her bag and finally finished with a bit of hand cleaner she also carried, and then felt her way back around to the front of the tree.

She had no idea which direction the van was in but, with her hands out, stepped forward the same number of paces she'd travelled to the tree. And felt open air. She turned in all directions, taking a step forward in each one, feeling empty air, then stepping back to her original spot. "Where are you?" she asked.

Silence. Surely she would have heard the van pull away!

She did a half turn to her left and took a few steps. More

open air. Maybe she should retrace her steps back to the tree. She tried that but the tree was no longer where she thought it should be, just more open space.

After several more attempts, and feeling completely disoriented, she stopped and let her arms drop to her sides, listening to the stillness, inhaling the forest scents of decomposing flora. The night offered only a waxing moon but she knew there would be stars, the light of either or both not enough to help her very limited vision.

Suddenly, she felt two icy hands at her waist. He leaned in from behind her and cool air hit her cheek as if a refrigerator had opened in the heat. He whispered in her ear, "You are helpless in the dark, *vrajitoarea*. Are you helpless in the daylight as well?"

That he'd been watching her struggle unnerved her. "I told you, I'm not a witch. I'm just a girl with psychic abilities," she blurted out.

"You intrigue me. I have not seen a *vrajitoarea* like you." He brushed her long red hair back from her neck and icy breath chilled her skin. A glacial tongue slowly dragged up her throat and then stopped below her ear, likely over a vein or artery.

"Careful, *nosferatu*. I wouldn't want to injure you."

"Careful, *vrajitoarea*, do not provoke me to injure you."

But he backed away slightly. Then, suddenly, he picked her up in his arms as if she weighed nothing and walked a few steps. Effortlessly, he leapt up into the back of the high vehicle. She felt herself lowered, deposited into a deep depression in the floor.

She heard the back door slam closed and then the remote lock the doors. It was pitch black, not even the potential of stars to offer any chance of illumination. She saw nothing, but the quiet shattered when he climbed in and lay immobile beside her, his cool body touching hers.

And she knew. This was the place he slept during the daylight hours, and she was here with him and would be until sunset. But she also realized something else: it wasn't near sunrise; it was still very dark outside! Why was he sleeping so soon?

When his cold hands reached for her, she understood.

He fondled her breasts through the fabric of her lacy blouse, but soon unlaced the corset she wore then raised the blouse and unhooked her bra. His cold lips found one of her nipples. She did not resist him; this too was her destiny, she understood that, and yet destiny was as cold as his flesh, as relentless, as pitiless.

As he sucked her nipple, she felt aroused and let herself sink into this new feeling—it was the easiest way. He got onto one knee—she felt his left leg move against her arm so that his foot was on the floor. Then he slid a hand beneath her waist and lifted her until she was propped against his bent leg like a doll, and all the while he fondled her flesh to firmness and beyond.

He lifted her skirt and slid a hand along the inside of her hot thigh to where her thighs met and she trembled. He pulled sharply at her panties, ripping out the crotch, and she gasped. Fingers stimulated her clitoris. She sighed and breathed heavily, sitting passively while he did what he wanted to her. Resistance, she felt, was indeed futile. He would more than overpower her and she knew he could hurt her badly.

When she was hot and moist, he lay her back down and himself on top; her body trembled. She could feel his cool penis against her leg. Suddenly, rapidly, he knocked her legs apart with his knees and positioned himself at her entrance and she had the sense that he was desperate for her warmth.

The second his flesh touched her labia, he jumped back with a cry as if he had again been electrocuted. "*Ce dracu ai fiuățit?*"

"I told you, *vampir*, you cannot penetrate me. Not unless I allow it. And I don't allow it."

He grabbed her arms and pulled her up and in the darkness she felt his cold breath like a blast of winter. "How *dare* you!" he hissed. "My ancestors were *voivode*. *I* am *voivode*! We are masters of all mortals, including you, vrajitoarea! I *will* have you! Open to me. Now!"

"I can't. And if you hurt me because I can't, I won't be able to help you. And then you'll never find him."

He paused for long moments, gripping her firmly, icy fingers digging into her arms as if he wanted to tear those limbs from her torso and dismember her. She could smell his breath and the metallic quality of the blood from his last feed. He wanted nothing more than to have her, her blood and her virginity, as he had no doubt had thousands of women in his centuries on this Earth, and he was not taking the unaccustomed rejection well.

In those moments when his penis touched her maidenhead, she'd had vision for one second, a blinding flash of vision, as if it were daytime and the sun shining. She saw him clearly, a glimpse of terrifying beauty and paleness, a look of fury and pain and desperation in his eyes. But despite all that, she could not allow him to penetrate her in this way either. Not now. If ever. Her greatest fear was that he would come to tolerate the physical pain of her rejection and take her anyway. And that would spell doom for both of them.

Suddenly he released her, snarling like an animal as he shoved her away from him. She fell back against the floor of this makeshift coffin knocking her skull on the wood. And she knew it was a coffin; in that precious second when she'd had vision, this is also what she saw: a large space as wide and long as the back of the van, as deep a pit as was possible to gouge into the chassis without hitting the ground. Like a cellar door that opens to a basement, this hole was his resting place where she was doomed to spend days until he and his foe finally clashed.

A loud crash made her jolt, but she quickly realized that he had pulled down the huge lid of this coffin to seal them in and protect him from daylight and intruders. But sealed in with him she was.

She thought about what would happen when he found the one he searched for. Everything would change. When that happened, she would see how destiny played itself out. The fate of the two undead. And her own fate.

As if reading her mind, he said, "Things will change between us, v*rajitoarea*, this I promise you."

For some reason, she said, "My name is Lorelei. You can call me Lora. Everyone does."

He made a small sound like a grunt and then, for no reason, she laughed into the darkness.

☦

She had been awake for hours, not used to sleeping for twelve in a row. And she had to pee. This wasn't a good arrangement for her, but then she knew he didn't give a damn about her comfort.

Lorelei thought a lot about the reading she'd done for his uncle. That vampire was vile; she felt that even before she began gazing into the ball. By comparison, at least Vlad—she had guessed his name and was pretty sure she was right, but even if she wasn't, the name fit—had some humanity lurking close to his crusty Lord-of-the-World veneer, if only she could reach it. It was crucial that she find the real *him*, for several reasons, all that her grandmother had predicted. But she knew she wasn't there by a mile. He was suspicious, paranoid, condescending, and liked to try to scare her into submission, but she wouldn't submit. She had to stay strong for both of them, although he didn't know that and even if she could get it across, he wasn't ready to hear the truth.

The truth. He was a victim of genes, an ancestry of rituals and customs that not only didn't suit his basic nature, which he was running fast from, but the family legacy would, without her help, destroy him. Even with her help he might be destroyed. And if he was, with him would go her one chance to be able to see again. But regaining vision was *her* destiny, so he wouldn't care about it. And she didn't want to reveal this because she hadn't swayed him yet and until she could, *if* she could, that was information she had better keep to herself so he wouldn't use it against her. And she didn't know how she could convey what she had learned about the path he was on because he wouldn't believe her: what she knew would challenge everything he accepted as true.

It was still early in this game, though. Tonight was night one of the search and it would take three nights of readings to find his uncle, of that she was certain. Three, that all-pervasive number of change that would allow the future to unfold. A future with a lot more involved than his battle and her resurrected vision.

☦

When the sun must have set, he roused. "Sleep well, *vampir*?" she asked, hardly able to keep the amusement out of her voice, which probably irritated him. But she had to have *some* fun!

"My rest is not your concern, v*rajitoarea*."

"Lorelei. My name is Lorelei. Lora."

Instead of responding, he got up, pushing the coffin lid as he rose. A rush of air streamed in and that refreshed her.

"I need a bathroom," she said.

He opened the back door and got out. Meanwhile, she struggled to sit then stand on limbs stiff from an extra four hours of immobility.

It was night, but there was a little light left in the sky and she could see a vague, blurry image of him waiting outside the vehicle for her. Tonight he didn't help her down but when she was out, instead of pointing her to the tree, he took her arm, slammed the rear door and remotely unlocked the other doors, leading her to the passenger side.

"Wait," she said, "I really do need a bathroom. And some food."

"We all need nourishment!" he snapped, and she realized that he was blood-starved. "There is a restaurant not far." Once they were on the road, they reached a small village within ten minutes, which she was thankful for. Twelve hours without a bathroom—it was a record she might submit to *The Guinness Book of World Records*!

At the *Kneipe*, he said, "The toilet is within, at the end of this row from the door. Wait here for me at this table by the window."

She hurried to the washroom and just made it in time. When she finished in the cubicle, she removed her clothes section by section and washed her body at the sink as best she could. She changed into the stretchy black dress and spare underwear and tossed the torn panties into the trash. She always carried an extra toothbrush and used it now. Her hair might be good for another day without washing, but after tonight... Well, she couldn't see it anyway. She combed it straight back and used a clip to hold it behind her head.

Refreshed, she headed into the beer hall/restaurant occupied by four customers and a stocky waitress, or at least those were the only forms her hazy vision could pick out.

At the outdoor table near the door, she asked the waitress if breakfast was served but, of course, this being Germany and this being not even a town but more a village and it was night too, there would be only some sort of wurst and sauerkraut and *kartoffelsalat* and gray bread. Plus beer. She ordered all that and waited.

She wasn't a prisoner. She could leave at any time. But she *was* a kind of prisoner, of fate. Fate, her Irish grandmother told her, is what will happen, regardless of what we want to happen and won't be much affected by what we do. *All we have control over is how we move towards it and how we react to it*, she'd said, and that made so much sense to Lorelei. She more or less knew where this situation would lead, but she didn't know the final outcome, for any of them.

While she plowed through the meat and sour cabbage, Vlad returned to the restaurant and sat across from her. The lighting was good enough that she could see through the outer edges of mildly hazy vision that he was not as pale as the last time she'd glimpsed him. He'd fed. She could smell the iron blood on him.

"How can you eat that?" he demanded. "It is disgusting. The look, the stench of cooked flesh."

"So is drinking blood to us mere mortals."

"You are a cannibal!"

"Carnivore. And I don't usually eat much meat but they didn't have anything else. I assume you want me alive so I can read for you."

He snorted.

She put down her fork and picked up the stein for another sip of beer. The beer was loosening her up, untying the knots of tension in her body, mind and soul. "Did you kill someone tonight?" She took another sip and waited. How he answered would be crucial.

"Why do you care?"

"Tell me." Then she added, "Please."

He paused but finally said, "I rarely kill. I do not need much blood and take only a small quantity. They might be weak but they are unharmed." And then, as if to justify what he probably saw as a weakness in himself, he added, "If I drained each night a mortal, there would be many bodies in every month and I do not wish to draw such attention to myself. My kind, we have been hunted over the centuries."

She nodded. She knew enough about vampire legends that it was clear his clan *had* been hunted, not so much in this century, but certainly the ones before now.

She deduced from how he told her this that he probably didn't kill at all, or hadn't since he'd been forced to. And he probably perceived that as a flaw in himself too when, in fact, it was his strength.

"Your father is a despot," she said. "The crystal told me

that. I imagine he insisted his sons learn to hunt to the death at an early age."

He said nothing so she knew she had hit the mark and could only imagine what it must have been like to be a child forced by a violent parent to kill someone for food.

Finally, she pushed the plate away, having eaten only half the meal. When the grim-voiced server returned, Lorelei told her in German that she wanted to take the rest of the food with her, and two large bottles of water. Then to Vlad she translated, "I'm taking the rest. And some water."

"Why?" he wanted to know when the waitress left with the plate. "You have just eaten and drunk."

She smiled. He was so naive. "You probably don't remember that we humans need to eat a couple of times a day, or night in this case. And I need water or I'll dehydrate. I doubt you'll want to stop again and besides, we're in Saxony, full of little places like this, and within an hour there won't be anything open."

When the waitress returned with the food and water, Lorelei reached into her bag for her wallet, but he had already pulled out some euros and tossed them onto the table and she didn't sense that he even glanced at the amount. "Come," he said, "it grows late."

They drove a short distance in the darkness and then he pulled off the road at a rest stop with picnic tables. He lifted her out of the seat and led her to a table. She heard night birds, bats maybe, soaring haphazardly overhead, and an owl hoot in the distance. The sweet scent of wildflowers permeated the air. There were cicadas in the grass—unusual for this region, but lately the temperature had soared beyond what was normal. The male insects scraped their hind legs together, trying to attract mates. The van was air conditioned and the contrast with the outside temperature staggered her

Once she was seated with him across from her, he said, "Read."

She pulled out the cloth and placed it over the table, smoothing it, then the holder on top and finally the crystal ball.

Without a word she motioned to him with her fingers and he placed his hands on the ball and hers went over his, which were tonight not cold but warm. *Only takes a little blood to humanize him*, she thought, then chided herself. *He's a vampire! He's not human. And don't take anything for granted.*

She stared into the crystal but this night the images were not quite as sharp as they had been the evening before. Still, she persevered, waiting for her inner vision to clear. Finally, something came to her, a place and with it a feel of torture and death that made her shudder. "He's in Hannover, on a street that... It's by the Leine River, where the Hannover Vampire dumped the remains of his victims."

"*Vampir!*" he sneered. "Fritz Haarmann was no *vampir*! He was a pedophile who killed boys. Twenty-seven."

"I don't know if your relative will be there when we arrive, but he's there right now. Maybe he's waiting for you."

"Come. We must hurry."

"Wait! That's not all I see. He's not alone. There's another vampire with him." She looked up at him. "One who looks like both him and you."

She sensed that he was startled by this, but he wouldn't convey that to her directly. Instead, he said again, "Come."

"Where are we now?" she asked when they were both in the van.

"Near Dresden."

"You went east instead of west." It sounded like a rebuke and she didn't want to be on his bad side, since she sensed his tension on the rise. She added quickly, "But you couldn't have known. Hannover has got to be over 300 kilometers from here. It must be close to midnight now. By the time we arrive and find him it could be 4:00 a.m. That doesn't leave you much time until sunrise."

He ignored her warning and drove at what felt like 160 KPH on the *autobahn* except where he had to slow to 120 or 100 because, her dad had explained, the speed limit was posted at that for some short stretches of road.

They arrived just outside Hannover before three in the morning and were soon driving along the Leine, where Friedrich Heinrich Karl 'Fritz' Haarmann with his lover, Hans Grans, had disposed of what remained of their victims after they'd sold the clothing and cooked the flesh, marketing the meat to the locals as pork.

"I do not sense him," Vlad said, "either of them. You are wrong."

"I don't think so. But he or they might have left. Stop so I can read the ball."

"No. There is no time."

She didn't argue with him. Clearly he was frustrated and agitated and possibly terrified of encountering his uncle and this other vampire, known or unknown. She reached into her bag and pulled out the Tarot deck, protected by the red velvet fabric she used. There wasn't space to do a real reading, but she shuffled the cards and concentrated her energy, then asked one question only: *Is there another vampire—besides the one seated next to me—here in Hannover?*

Then she selected a card. "Turn on the light," she said. "I can't see the card."

"You cannot see at all!" he snapped.

Instead of flipping on the vehicle light, he snatched the card from her hand. "It reads Five of Cups. If that means anything." He tossed the card at her and she had to feel around for it.

"It means he's not here. Neither of them is. It's a card of loss. You've lost both vampires. It's a quagmire you're in, one that you won't get out of soon.

"*Fiu de cătea!*" He stopped the vehicle and turned on her. "This is your fault!"

"No, Vlad, it's not!" It was the first time she'd called him by that name and since he didn't correct her, she knew it was accurate. "You were impatient. You wouldn't let me read to see which way to go, so you went the wrong way. And I warned you he might be gone when we arrived. Why would he stay in one place, since he's running from you as much as waiting for you? He's probably trying to lure you somewhere, maybe with this other vampire. This quest of yours requires some finesse and you've got to be patient." She reached over to touch his arm. "I know you're worried—"

He slapped her hand away as if she was an insect then snarled like a wolf in her direction. "V*rajitoarea*, you may count yourself fortunate if I do not strangle you this night!"

She turned from him and stared out the window, although she couldn't see much. There were very dim yellow streetlamps along the river road, placed close to what might be a stone fence; not much to help her see. There didn't seem to be much to help her at all. "I'm sorry," she said in a small voice, not an apology to him but one to herself. "I need to focus more, see if I can get a better sense of things. This is so complicated. And I'm not seeing the crystal as well as I should."

She turned back to him. "Tomorrow is another night. We're close, I can feel that. It's unlikely he travelled further than we did distance-wise, neither of them could have. You'll find the one you're seeking. I saw that much when I first read you. I'll help you."

He sat for a minute then put the van in gear and turned back, driving at a less frantic pace, leaving the city behind until he found a road and started down it.

Like the night before, they were in a small clearing. Everything was a repeat of the previous evening, including what happened in the coffin, even to him ripping out the crotch of her panties and she realized she had no clean spares and would have to go without from now on.

Tonight he was more aggressive with her, his hands determined, his lips doing things to her flesh that she did not know could produce sensations. She sensed he was not as cautious about the shock he would get, either at her throat or at her labia.

What he did to her body over the last hours of darkness filled her with nearly unbearable heat and she trembled uncontrollably with desire until she thought she might explode or burst into flame and it was all she could do to keep her wits about her. Despite him being such an ass, he knew his way around flesh and she could barely keep from begging him to take her. He must have sensed this because at the same moment his penis touched her hymen, his teeth touched the skin over her jugular. He intended to pierce her in both places at once!

On contact, he blasted back and away from her and, as he did, she had the most astonishing view of the world since she had been a child and lost her full sight. As if a light had been turned on, her vision cleared perfectly, for what must have been three or four seconds, enough to let her investigate his beautiful, sensitive face, his pain, his fury, his desperation. That image of him lingered when her sight again faded to normal as her body quivered with awe and astonishment and the deep yearning for him that also stayed with her.

He leapt up and opened the back door, clearly needing air or to at least get away from her. And before he slammed the door closed, she saw at the edges of what vision she possessed just a little bit of the outside darkness.

She lay panting, her naked body throbbing and aching with a longing that was new to her and one that would remain unfulfilled. For now. Perhaps forever. Then she laughed grimly and whispered into the darkness, "Maybe I'll die a vestal virgin."

When he finally returned, he lay next to her, not touching her, and she heard the lid close.

From the quiet darkness, he asked in a civil tone, "Why does this happen?"

She knew what he meant but didn't know what to tell him, or how much to tell him. "I'm not sure," she said, struggling to think of some explanation that bore a semblance of truth and that would be enough to satisfy him. But no words came to her.

"Know this, v*rajitoarea*: I *will* have you!"

The determination in his voice held the confidence of the high born. He was used to getting his way and would find a route around this barrier. *Maybe you will*, she thought. *But maybe you won't.*

⸸

When night again descended, he rose quickly and told her to dress. They drove away immediately, headed back to Hannover and to the same river road.

"I need the usual amenities," she said.

He didn't respond but seemed intent on searching for something.

"Food. A bathroom. You know, human things. And you might want a new reading, just in case you're still searching for your uncle and want to head the right way." Okay, she should not have teased him, but he was always so serious!

Suddenly he braked hard and within a second had leapt out of the vehicle. She saw his shape vaguely in the sky's fading twilight. He walked quickly towards the water and bent down.

Lorelei fumbled in her bag for the Tarot, hoping to find out what was going on, but before she could get the cards unwrapped he was back in the van, tossing something onto the dashboard.

"What's that?" she asked.

"Bone." His voice was tight.

That left her speechless. Maybe the one he was searching for was dead. Could that be?

He turned the vehicle sharply and headed back the way they'd come.

"What's going on?" she asked.

He said nothing.

"Tell me. I can help you."

Silence.

He drove a short way and pulled into a campground. The attendant at the gate said, "*Es gibt viele freie Campingplätze.*" Vlad clearly didn't understand him, so she translated: "He says the camp is almost empty, nearly deserted."

The attendant named the price and Vlad paid it silently,

then drove through the woods. Off in the distance she saw a light that she thought might be a bonfire.

Finally he stopped and said, "The lake is there, if you wish to bathe and relieve yourself."

Tonight he didn't help her; he disappeared. She managed to get herself out of the van by easing her body down the side of the seat until her toes touched the ground, which was a long way. She heard water gently splashing against rocks on the shore and with her hands out in front of her, headed in that direction, taking very small and careful steps, not knowing what was on the ground ahead of her.

She tripped once over what might have been a tree root, but the water sounded closer and finally she sensed it was within a step or two.

Lorelei backed up two steps and crouched down, feeling around her until she located a rock, high enough and dry enough to leave her sandals and dress and the shoulder bag on, everything but the ruined underwear which she balled up to toss next time she found a trash can.

Then she turned towards the water, feeling pebbles underfoot that bothered her. Generally her balance was good but not on surfaces like this and on unfamiliar terrain.

She moved carefully, feeling the cold water cover her ankles then quickly rise up to her thighs. The floor of this lake was also full of pebbles and she hoped none would cut her feet. She didn't want the injury and she also didn't want him smelling her blood.

Eventually she was forced to let go and allow herself to float then submerge briefly. Her head surfaced and the bracing water was both enlivening and comforting and she felt happy to have the lake holding her up. Above, she saw a gauze-covered waxing moon that provided little light but enough that she could see the surface of the lake where it reflected.

She swam along that lighted path easily—something she'd learned to do before she was blinded—and ducked her head repeatedly to get as much of the grit out of her hair as possible without shampoo. Swimming was a pleasure, a freedom, one of the things she could do with almost no effort and, due to not seeing, nearly everything she did required a lot of effort.

Soon she felt cold and realized it was time to get out of the water. She circled, needing to make sure she was going towards land and not further out. Trees back from the shore that she could see as dark shadows against the less-dark night pointed her to land and she headed that way along the water-path of reflected moonlight.

Slowly she made her way from the lake, water dripping off her body. The air chilled her and she shivered. She wished she had a towel. She ran her hands back through her hair, squeezing out the excess moisture, then slid them down her arms, legs, back, stomach, trying to sluice away the drops that remained.

Suddenly he was there, before her, hot hands roaming over her cool, wet flesh, her arms, her breasts, her hips, which he pulled into his. In an incomprehensible moment, he kissed her mouth, forcing her lips apart to admit his hot tongue. He wrapped warm arms around her, and although she still shivered a little, she didn't feel as cold. He was warmer than the night air; he must have fed.

But he didn't go further this time. Instead, he told her, "Put on your clothing."

Her body was still wet but she took the dress he handed her and pulled it over her head, slipped on the sandals and pulled her dripping hair back into a ponytail, tying and knotting the hair around itself. He took her arm to lead her away.

"Wait! Where's my bag?"

"I have," he said, and that made her uncomfortable. She did not like letting it out of her hands and definitely not with someone else, mortal or immortal.

He led her to a picnic table.

"I'll need my bag," she said, a touch of hysteria in her voice that she knew he heard.

"What will you barter for it?"

"If you're asking if I'll exchange my blood and my virginity for the bag, no. But you might want to consider that without the tools of my trade, I can't aid you."

They both paused over this stalemate. When he handed the bag across the table, relief washed through her.

As before, she placed the cloth and set up the holder and ball and his hands went to the last, hers over his.

Tonight she had a hard time seeing images. Time elapsed until he said tensely, "Why do you wait? Read!"

"I'm trying," she said, knowing that something had changed because the images should have been clear by now. "Sometimes it takes a while." But it had never taken this long. She worried that the more he tried to penetrate her and the longer her vision cleared with that contact, the less she could see in the ball. Was she losing her prophetic abilities?

Finally, something swirled, and, relaxing, she exhaled the breath she'd been holding...until she saw what it was and gasped. "I...I see only one vampire now. The other one is—"

"Extinguished. I know this. Where is the one remaining?"

She looked at him, viewing an opaque darkness against a slightly less-dark background. "The other vampire who looks like you both...that's your uncle? Was he killed?"

He didn't answer but she felt his tension.

"Was that...part you fished out of the Leine the dead one?"

"It is the bone of *vampir*."

"Was he killed by your un—"

"Stop asking questions! Read! Where can I find the one who remains?"

His tone was savage and Lorelei bent her head over the crystal, hoping answers would emerge. And they did. "He's in Düsseldorf. Standing in front of the apartment building where the house was that the Vampire of Düsseldorf lived in."

"Another *vampir* poseur!" he snapped, pulling his hands away and standing. "Come!"

Once they were seated in the van, she said, "I have to eat something."

He tossed a paper bag onto her lap. She opened it to find *frikadelle* on a bread roll with mustard and devoured most of the traditional meatball sandwich, taking a huge swallow of water from one of the bottles she'd stuffed into her bag. She wondered where he'd gotten the food but figured he stole it from the camper whose blood was warming him now.

On the two-and-a-half-hour drive to Düsseldorf, she pushed the buds into her ears and listened to another chapter from the audio book on blood drinkers.

The Vampire of Düsseldorf—Peter Kürten—started young. His home was an incestuous one and he followed in his abusive father's footsteps. That led him to torturing animals and murdering a ten-year-old girl. Ultimately, he married and his wife turned him in when the police were hot on his trail. Kürten confessed to seventy-nine murders and was executed.'

It didn't go unnoticed by Lorelei and probably not by Vlad either that this uncle of his was hitting all the vampire hot spots in Germany. There must be a message in that, but she didn't know what it could be. So she asked.

"Why do you think he's in these places where vampires lived."

"They were not *vampirii*."

"Okay, vampire wannabes."

"He mocks me." He sounded bitter. "It is his way. He is telling me he is stronger, I am like these mortal males, a fraud. He believes I am incapable of defeating him."

"Do you really think that's what he's saying?"

"Yes. I am certain."

"How well do you know him?"

"I have known him since birth."

There was a lull in the conversation until Lorelei said, "So, do you have siblings?"

He hesitated. "What is *siblings*?"

"Brothers and sisters in your family."

"There are no sisters in my family."

That was odd and gave her pause. "So..." she said slowly, "no females were born."

"I did not say that."

She was almost afraid to ask, but knowledge was everything. "They weren't allowed to live."

"Yes."

Shocked, she asked, "Why?"

"Because females are inferior."

Her eyebrows shot up, her jaw dropped open and her eyes widened. She blinked a few times in disbelief. That explained a *lot*.

Finally she managed, "So, there are women, your mother, for example, otherwise you wouldn't have been born, or is there something I don't know about the birth of a vampire."

"A *vampir* may create one such as himself, but for the strongest, a male impregnates a mortal female. She provides offspring who turn to their innate nature at some point in time, then the female becomes unnecessary."

"You mean she's killed."

"It is her honor to increase our line."

"Some honor!" she snapped. "You know, you and your line have a barbaric and antediluvian attitude about a lot of things, and about women in particular. It's pretty absurd, not to mention repugnant, and makes your whole nest of bloodsuckers look like something that should have died out a long time ago."

He said nothing, and she was just as glad. She didn't want to argue equality with him right now, but she was female and this attitude not only made her furious but wouldn't bode well for her. She'd already felt the essence of it from him. He treated her as an inferior and it rankled him that he needed her psychic skills. He saw her as a possession, to be used for blood and sex, a possession he could get rid of when he grew bored. At best she was a pet that he liked to caress on occasion. She knew she was meant to serve a purpose that went beyond that and it was only her psychic abilities that had spared her life until now. But for how much longer? Oddly, by verbalizing his beliefs, it steeled her against him. Yes, she would help him, but that was all. He would find more resistance in the coffin at sunset. *If* he lived that long.

She didn't speak to him again until they arrived in Düsseldorf, when she asked, "What time is it?"

He pressed a button on the van's dash. "Twenty-one hundred hours."

"If you pull over, I can see where he is, unless you want to just drive around the city all night hoping to run into him."

He parked, leaving the vehicle running, and she set up the ball between them. Now the images came clearer and she knew that was a direct result of her revised feelings about him; she was no longer so vulnerable.

"He's gone," she said. "I'll have to read this later, or tomorrow night to find out where. There's no information right now."

His fist slammed the steering wheel and she heard plastic crack.

Silently, he spent the next couple of hours pointlessly driving around the city. Finally she said, "You must be able to sense that he's not here."

"Yes. And?" His impatience was like an assault.

She shook her head. He was a stupid, stubborn idiot. Even though he knew the vampire had gone, he wouldn't give up. Then it occurred to her that he probably needed something to do so he wouldn't lose it.

Finally he demanded, "Read again. This time, I want to know where he is *now*!"

He pulled to the curb and she set up as before. The ball wouldn't tell her much. "I need to read this somewhere else. There are too many emotions in this vehicle. I need a cleaner, purer space."

He snarled something in Romanian, turned the van and pulled out quickly, causing a car coming up from behind to screech to a halt.

They may have passed this way before, she wasn't sure. He stopped and then yanked her impatiently out of the vehicle and led her into a park. Although late, it was humid and there were people sitting or walking. He held her around the waist, *keeping me from fleeing!* she thought, but more likely to present them as a couple, which would draw less suspicion, although they both wore black clothing and that, alone, evoked hesitation in Germany.

"*Guten abend!*" she called, smiling in the general direction of what were probably older people she sensed passing by or seated on benches, who replied in kind. He, of course, said nothing.

Finally they reached a fountain and guiding her he said, "Sit on the ledge," which she did, feeling droplets of cool spray on the back of her arm. He sat to her right. She looked around but no one appeared to be seated nearby, or close enough to know what they were doing, but she couldn't be sure. This park had ornate streetlamps with dim bulbs. Above, what moon there was had moved across the sky, poised behind her, blocked by the tall, ancient oaks.

Once the ball was in place and his hands on it, she peered down into the crystal. The images swirled and finally came to rest, forming a picture that she spoke in words. "He's headed north. Maybe back to Hannover, I don't know."

"He would not return there."

While she waited for more images to appear, suddenly he said, "I know where he is going. Come."

She followed him to the van and once they were pulling away she asked, "Want to let me in on the destination?"

"Schleswig."

She had heard of this place but had no idea where it was. A quick typing of the letters SCH in the search bar of the vampire audio book brought her to this, which she listened to and then paraphrased aloud for him, paragraph by paragraph: "Schleswig is in the Schleswig-Holstein region; the capital is Kiel. It's close to the border with Denmark."

She glanced at him but he didn't turn her way, just kept driving at a breakneck speed that might end up killing them both, well, her anyway.

"King Abel was a Dane who was gung-ho about hunting. He got the throne away from his brother by committing fratricide, chopping off his sibling's head to be exact. He married a German, Mechtild von Holstein, and they had four kids. He died in some battle or other but wouldn't stay dead so they staked his corpse in the heart. Now he's on what we call in Germany *Wilde Jagd* which means the *Wild Hunt*, kind of supernatural spirits that tend to appear with horses from hell, demon hounds, blowing magic horns, haunting the countryside on one of these wild hunts...you probably get the picture. He's most often after girls to capture, but anybody who sees him dies, and especially anybody who goes up against him. But you knew about him, didn't you? That's how you know your uncle is in Schleswig. Another vampire spot in Germany."

"Another *fake vampir*. This one did not even drink blood like the other two."

"Yeah, well, I guess it was the stake through the heart business that defined him back in the day. Why is your relative picking all these vampire spots?"

"I told you why."

"You did, but it doesn't make sense. There's more to it

than this. I think I should read the ball again."

"I will not stop! Schleswig is five hours from here. I know he will be there. I want this over."

Lorelei did too, but not quite this way. She felt there was more to this strange quest than she understood right now. And she did not trust this uncle. Not at all.

When he had come into the tent at the festival, he'd brought a malevolent energy with him that made her want to run screaming. Fortunately, it was at the start of the festival and a lot of people wanted readings. She had a couple sit on the cot and wait while she read for the vampire. They had music player buds in their ears and the vampire kept the conversation low.

"I search for one like myself, *vrajitoarea*. Or do you prefer the German word *hexe*?" he said.

She did not bother to tell him she wasn't a witch. She knew that if he could have mesmerized her, he would have, if she could see, but she could not, and he noticed that right away. "Your second sight saves you," he noted. "If your eyes saw mine, you would already be submissive to my power."

She read the crystal and discovered the existence of Vlad, who he identified as his nephew, his brother's third son. One of the two remaining sons. He said he was going to kill him.

"But why?" she asked, not able to help the question.

"That is not your concern. You, *vrajitoarea*, you will bring him to me."

Lorelei paused. Though she couldn't see him, she felt

almost a psychic wall in front of her, as real as any of brick and mortar. But she wasn't a witch. She didn't know anything about protective spells, if it was a protective spell and not just super defensiveness. And though she couldn't see him visually, instinctively she sensed that she had to be careful. He would kill her and everyone nearby. "I won't lead anyone to their death, even a vampire," she said.

He laughed, a chilling sound that rattled her. "You will. He will insist on it. As I insist. You have no choice but to lead him to slaughter by my hand."

"Why do you want to kill him?" she asked again.

His cold hand took one of hers and he turned it over, bringing the inside of her wrist to his icy lips. She felt his teeth touch her skin and then he simultaneously jerked back and dropped her hand as if it was on fire. He jumped to his feet, turned and stormed out of the tent, taking with him a sensation of long-dead air and burial dirt.

Instantly she realized she'd been set up. As her grandmother had told her long ago, the undead would find her, and she had mentioned the number two. Lorelei would be under their command and she must bear it with dignity. It would be violent and it would be fatal, and her grandmother wouldn't say for who, her or them or all of them. She must persevere to the end. Her own salvation depended on it.

She turned towards Vlad and said quietly, "This is not as you imagine. There are things you don't know, Vlad. I can't articulate them, but I sense there's a lot of danger for you and you need help to face it. Please, let me help you."

She didn't know why she said that. He didn't look at her. She wasn't even sure he had heard her, let alone was considering her sincere offer.

Ahead was a sign and as they passed it she glimpsed it quickly out of the corner of her eye when the headlights hit it. Despite the blurry vision, she *thought* it read *Kiel—50 KLM*. If that was accurate, they would arrive at Schleswig within the hour. It was already late. By sunrise Vlad might be dead, and so might she.

Suddenly, he pulled off to the side of the road, put the van in park but left the engine running. He stared out the windshield and said quietly, "Read."

Despite the intensity of emotions and other vibrations in the vehicle, she knew he wouldn't get out, so she set up and watched the inside of the crystal until she was finally able to say, "He's going to trick you. You have to be careful because what he tells you is a lie but there is underlying truth, and you'll feel that truth and respond to it. He wants your blood to prove something...to your father." She saw something else in the crystal and couldn't quite believe it. "King Abel is riding tonight. The hunt will be wild. And fatal."

He waited a few moments before slipping his hands out from under hers. She felt him staring at her face, as if he wanted to say something but couldn't. Finally he turned, shifted into gear and drove quickly into the city to face his fate, and bring her to her own.

✠

Schleswig-Holstein was wild forests and neat farmland, the latter dotted with black and white cows, the breed taking their name from this region. She did not see this but sensed most of it and smelled the rest.

As they neared the town of Schleswig, she asked, "How will you know where he is?"

"I know."

He drove through the city which she could not see, but she had listened to the audio book on the way. Orderly and antique German, with buildings hundreds of years old in a row, roofs various heights, painted lovely colors, pristine, early flowers everywhere. It sounded nice. Not the kind of town where a murder of the undead would take place.

The city was small and they arrived and left within minutes. "Where are we going?" she asked.

He didn't answer.

She knew a *Wilde Jagd* never took place in a populated area, but always in the forest, hunting land, and that, she also knew from her last crystal reading, was where this showdown would occur.

Eventually he turned from the main road and onto a smaller, rougher one and at some point stopped the van. He switched off the ignition and said, "You will remain here."

"I think you need me to come—"

"I said, remain here!"

He waited until finally she answered, "Alright," before opening the door, getting out and closing it sharply after him.

Lorelei sat in the van chewing her nails. What happened

here was going to impact on her. She couldn't just sit around waiting! She could tell from the last reading that once he heard a semblance of what would sound like truth, part of him would be in shock. That's what his opponent wanted.

She opened the door and slid out and down to the ground carefully, closing the door quietly, carrying the heavy bag slung across her shoulder. It was dark in this woodsy area—the scent of trees, wild flowers with decay hanging heavy in the air.

She had no idea which way he had gone and listened to see if she could catch any sounds at all. Maybe that was something, just ahead, but she wasn't sure because it was so hard to know which direction a sound was coming from. *This is stupid! How can I find them?* she thought. *You can't*, she assured herself, *at least not by thinking about it.*

She pulled the ball from the bag and held it between her hands, her head bowed as she stared into it, seeing nothing for what felt like forever, then an image formed, a figure, and it was almost as if the image directed her by pointing.

Lorelei began to walk, leaves crackling and twigs snapping underfoot. Soon she heard voices, familiar ones, and as she neared, the one who had come to her first at the music festival switched from Romanian to English because he had obviously heard or seen her and wanted her to know something. "And the *vrajitoarea* arrives in time to hold your hand as you die!"

"It is you who will die tonight!" That was Vlad's voice, sounding confident.

"Ask the *vrajitoarea*, little brother. She knows."

Lorelei stopped in her tracks, obeying the image in the crystal to halt. The image of her grandmother.

Little brother? This was Vlad's older brother? But it was the same voice, the same energy she had met in the tent. He had lied to her, saying he was Vlad's uncle. And the bone—that had to be the uncle, and the brother killed him! Did Vlad know that his uncle had been murdered? He must.

And now, in a moment of clarity, she understood King Abel. He cut off the head of his brother to get the throne. This is what Vlad's brother intended to do. She had to warn Vlad! But how?

"It is tradition, youngest brother. Only one can survive to overthrow the ruler and be king. Our father knows this. With our middle brother gone and now his brother also, that leaves only me and you to challenge him. And soon there will be only me."

"I have no wish to be king."

"Then why are you here? Why did you not run off as is your way with the *vrajitoarea*? She is willing to go with you, not that her consent matters. Although perhaps for you it does?" He said the last in a scathing tone.

Vlad hesitated. She could feel his confidence teeter. And she also felt him change direction, not wanting to get sucked into an argument that required him to defend himself. "Why do you not just kill our father, then? Take the throne of bones. Who cares? Why drag me into this?"

The eldest brother laughed, a sound that rang of the

howling of hounds from hell. Instantly, the wind picked up as if a brewing storm had suddenly turned aggressive and all around her tree branches whipped the increasingly cool air.

Like a dog with a bone, the brother kept gnawing at the tender spot. "You are naive, young brother, truly the weakest one. You could not take her. This shows your true colors. You are inferior stock, the son of our mother not our father. You are pathetic!" the brother shouted, digging into a couple more sore points at once, hoping to destroy Vlad's confidence completely.

Lorelei was having trouble keeping her balance in what had become a gale. She knew the brother spoke in English because he wanted her to hear everything. And now she trembled at what he said next. "When you are dust, impotent brother, I will take her, and for me it will be easy. And why not? She is not too homely, and she will likely breed well."

Now, more than ever, it was crucial that she find a way to help Vlad. She couldn't think what to do and staring in the ball produced only the same figure, of her grandmother, still, waiting, what Lorelei was being instructed to do. And yet she couldn't wait.

"Don't listen to him!" she cried. "It's a trick to make you question yourself, so he can get you when you're down."

The brother laughed again and the storm picked up as if in response. Was it reality, what she had read, that vampires can control the elements?

"The *vrajitoarea* wishes to save you. She believes you

are the gentler *vampir*, the one who will treat her well. That you can love her. She is too dim to realize we *vampirii* are incapable of love. Besides, you are feeble; even she is stronger than you, and she knows that. And I am much stronger than you both, and stronger than our ancient father, whose time has passed. I have killed many and understand death in a way you do not. I am the only one who can defeat our father. But to do that, I must first kill you! It is required."

Suddenly, amidst the sounds of the storm, she could swear she heard horses' hooves. The wind screamed, wild beasts roaring, and a loud yet dull sound echoed around her, like a hunting horn. She trembled in terror when other sounds filled the cold air, close by, too close. Snarling, growling, mad dogs fighting. Not dogs, wolves!

The battle had begun and she could only struggle to remain standing, listening to rending and tearing, teeth gnashing, yelping, feral animals in a battle to the death, tearing into one another without mercy. Then she heard metal clanking against metal, like swords, and the louder sound of horses' hooves racing ever nearer.

King Abel has come to hunt, she thought. *And thank the gods and goddesses that I cannot see this!* If the legends were true, if she saw the King, she would be abducted or killed.

She screamed into the wind, "Remember how Abel killed his brother!" Her voice lashed back at her, and she doubted Vlad had heard. And what she wanted to say was that Abel's brother had cut off his head, but Vlad's brother had done the same thing already, in a different way, digging into insecurities and self-doubts, cutting off Vlad's reason, leaving him vulnerable.

The hurricane-force winds knocked her off her feet and she clutched the ball as she fell. The ground beneath her shook as if the earth quaked. Suddenly a shocked cry cut the night air. One had been injured. Badly. The words "*Mori!*" split the darkness, and she didn't know which of them had uttered this demand but she understood from the term *memento mori* the meaning: *Die!*

As if a door had slammed shut, the wind stopped and all sound ceased but for what came from her. She gasped in air, nearly hyperventilating. Her body trembled beyond what she could control.

Suddenly, she heard sucking sounds, lapping, and knew instinctively that the victor was taking the spoils, the blood of the defeated.

A long time elapsed with only this sound in the silence surrounding her, or so it felt like, then she sensed movement. The survivor stalked her, crunching leaves underfoot, and her body throbbed with terror. *Please, grandmother, help me if you can!* she prayed silently.

Hands grasped her by the upper arms and swiftly yanked her to her feet. She knew her face reflected the panic she felt. She couldn't speak.

A mouth found hers, one that tasted of wet blood, and she nearly gagged. Hands, hot as fire, pulled her clothes from her body. She heard a zipper lowered and then she was lifted by the backs of her thighs and felt his hard erection at her opening, felt him ready to jam her body onto his and rip her childhood away. Even then, his teeth found her throat and hot breath seared her skin as his mouth located the perfect position for his incisors to stab her vein.

"No!" she cried. "Not like this. Not yet. It's not over! Vlad, wait! Please, you've got to wait!"

He struggled against the force that came from her keeping him at bay. She did not know where this strength originated but thought her grandmother's spirit had to be helping her. She experienced pressure against her hymen and pressure at her neck at the same time. With only a little more effort he would pierce her. She had to stay strong.

She thought of her grandmother and cried out, "*Go bhfóire Dia orainn!*"

A surge of energy burst from her and while he was not shoved away and he did not retreat, he could not go further. Then, she felt one of his sharp canines just scrape the flesh of her neck and his lips latch onto her throat taking this surface blood.

She let him drink it. All her energy was focused on avoiding something more dangerous.

He sucked at the skin until it became painful; a bruise would form, if not something worse. She wondered if the scrape would become infected.

Slowly he lowered both of them to the forest floor. It began to rain but he didn't seem to notice. He clamped his arms around her, holding her close in a vice grip. What he was doing reminded her of a baby sucking breast milk, and she felt his vulnerability even as she sensed the violence in him that had yet to abate. He had murdered his brother, this vampire who did not kill. He must be starting to feel himself a pawn in a larger game. He needed comforting, and he needed more, but she couldn't give him more, not if she wanted to save herself.

Even this abrasion of her skin let her see again for all the moments the surface blood flowed from her to him. The world around her sharpened: trees became defined against the night sky, their colors shades of grey; raindrops sparkled beneath the gibbous moon, a brilliant prism of light. A low, white cloud floated in the darkness above.

And then she spotted the headless corpse of Vlad's oldest brother lying on the grass at the edge of the clearing and she gasped.

Her eyes searched the ground until she located the head resting just beside them, clearly torn from the torso. She saw elongated incisors in the gaping mouth. The eyes had gone flat, with no sign of life, and yet they stared in her direction as if accusing her from beyond the grave.

Seeing this monstrous head so close unnerved her and her concentration slipped.

Vlad's teeth instinctively cut deeper.

She propelled herself to consciousness, to control, and closed her eyes, erecting a steel barrier between the two of them; his teeth did not make it to the vein.

He sucked absently, as if he was asleep, unaware of what he was doing. Her neck had become painfully sore and finally she said softly, like a mother talking to a very young child, "Vlad, we need to leave here. We need to go inside the vehicle. You need rest."

At first he didn't seem to hear her but when she repeated what she'd said, he stirred. "Come," she said, making an effort to extricate herself from his embrace, and he released her. Gently but firmly she pushed his shoulders back and heard a loud pop as suction broke and his lips left her skin. Her flesh throbbed and tingled painfully. "Come," she said again, finding the crystal, taking his hand, leading him away as if he were a child.

He let go of her hand for a second and stepped back, bending, and she knew he had grabbed the head, likely by the long, dark hair, and she was horrified; he wanted to bring it with them!

When they reached the vehicle, by feel Lorelei led him to the driver's door and said, "Leave that in here, please."

Silently he opened the door and placed the head of his brother onto the driver's seat. She closed the door and pulled him by the arm to the back of the vehicle, opened the door and he lifted her up and in.

From the moment he stopped sucking at the scrape on her neck, tasting her blood, her vision had begun to fade, so much so that she couldn't see him now. She couldn't see anything.

He lay down beside her, his body curled, nearly a fetal position, and she wrapped her arms around him. He didn't respond or react, and it was as if he was in a deep sleep, or a coma.

They were both wet, their clothing soaked, and Lorelei hoped she wouldn't get sick from this chilly rain. More, she hoped he would recover quickly from this trauma. What she told him was true. This wasn't over. There was one more relative to confront.

⊕

The following night Vlad left the van to walk in the woods alone.

Lorelei did the things she had to but she needed food. It felt like quite a while since she'd eaten and swallowed the last drops of bottled water.

He was away a long time, many hours. Her stomach cramped from hunger and her throat became parched. More than that, the skin on her neck he had sucked continuously for so long felt swollen and tender to the touch and she feared that without applying something antibacterial she would be in trouble. This was one time she wished she was a witch and knew about herbs.

He returned late, morning just a few hours away. Silently, he took her arm and led her to the vehicle, lifting her to the seat. She wondered if the brother's head was still with them and even though she couldn't smell decay, she knew the head was there—she would have heard Vlad open the driver's door if he'd removed it.

"I need food and water," she said.

He didn't answer, just started the vehicle.

"I need something soon. I feel ill." She felt she had to stress this because he didn't seem to be aware of her. She knew she could not go through another night of hunger and thirst without dire consequences.

There would be no restaurant or food store open at this hour, but he found a late-night *tankstelle* in the capital of Kiel. She bought several litre bottles of water, two cups of coffee, and all the snack food she could carry. She asked the gas station clerk in German if he sold anti-bacterial ointment and he handed over a tube of something she couldn't see.

"*Wieviel*?" she asked, but Vlad had already tossed euros onto the counter and took her arm, moving her outside and back to the van.

So far, he hadn't spoken one word. Something had been knocked out of him by the fight, and she wasn't sure what. While she ate some of the salty snack food and gulped water then coffee, back and forth, she thought about this silence and what it could mean.

She knew he was sensitive, he just had trouble showing it. He could hardly speak, as if he had been taught not to. Coming from such a violent macho family, that was understandable. His brother had forced him into a fight but he might not see it that way. He had murdered his brother—anyone, living or undead, would be traumatized. Maybe he thought he should have found a path around this situation, and she entertained the idea that maybe he could have. The circumstances were slightly beyond her understanding, so she wasn't certain what was and what was not possible. He likely berated himself for being gullible. She wondered how much he knew. Without him telling her, she could only speculate, and that, she realized, might lead her in the wrong direction.

The second she had eaten all four bags of chips, two of pretzels and a packet of nuts and finished off one of the large bottles of water, she wiped her hands on the velvet cloth in her bag and pulled out the crystal ball.

He seemed disinterested. Normally, she felt him at least glance in her direction from time to time, but not tonight.

She placed her hands on the sides and was surprised to see her grandmother's image still there. *What should I do, grandmother?* she asked. *How can I help him? Help both of us?*

The image swirled for a time and then stopped. Lorelei could see that despite her strong desire to direct events, the image warned that she couldn't. Everything lay in the hands of this one next to her who was so brutalized and brutalizing. She had to trust him to find the right path. But she wasn't sure she could. Everything about him was contradictory. She didn't know which part of him to believe in, and then it occurred to her that she had to believe in all parts. He was a killer and a benevolent dictator. Sensitive and insensitive at the same time. Was he destined to rule or destined to succumb to the rule of another? Could he meet this last challenge? She didn't know and that frightened her because whatever happened, she, too, was only a pawn in this game of dominance.

Other images swirled in the crystal and she soon realized where they were headed. Her cell phone battery was dead so she had to ask him, "How far?"

He didn't answer her.

A quick mental calculation assured her that it had to be around 2,000 kilometers from where they were to Transylvania. It would take them several nights of driving. She hoped he would recover in time to face his father. He had to.

☦

As they crossed Germany, the Czech Republic, a corner of Austria and then passed through Hungary, Vlad was silent, lost in his own world. Whenever she asked a question, he didn't answer. Sometimes she just talked, for the sake of hearing a voice. If he was aware of what she said, he didn't let on. *He's in some sort of catatonic state*, she thought, *but one where he can still function.*

They stopped for food—for both of them—and for her to wash up. He drove for hours, though, and it was only her pleas about her physical needs which included getting out to walk a bit, or the need for gas, that made him pull off the highway.

During the day hours he slept next to her, careful not to touch her, which was very different from how it had been. She had the sense he was wounded, maybe his pride, probably something deeper, and that he was not up to facing more rejection.

She'd been afraid to talk about what happened, and what was to come. But as they entered Romania, and then headed up the mountains for the very central area of this most wild and well-fortified land that time paid little attention to, she realized that she had to speak now. Later might be too late.

"I didn't know he was your brother," she said. "He told me he was your uncle, and the crystal just said he was a liar and that he wanted to kill you. But he also *told* me he wanted to kill you. I also saw that he was a fraud, but I didn't know exactly how. And dangerous. He said I had to bring you to him. He demanded it but, more, you would demand it, and I would be compelled to do it.

"I know he said things to hurt you, to make you feel weak. But Vlad, you have to understand something. All that's happened, with him, between us, it's not your fault. Or mine. This is destiny. You have yours and I have my own destiny to fulfill, and our fates are linked. That's why you can't have me. Why your brother couldn't either. Or your real uncle, if I'd met him. I'm only stronger than you in this one way and it's because I need to be. I need to help you to help myself."

He said nothing and she wondered if he'd even heard her let alone understood.

"One thing your brother said was true, about dethroning your father. There can only be one king, but you know that already. He told you that and that part of what he said is real. I don't know why it's this way with your kind, but it must have always been so: a battle that eliminates contenders for the throne until only one is left; taking a woman to increase your line then doing away with her and any girl children; living in isolation out of fear of being hunted by both mortals and your own kind; fear of the intimacy that can develop between equals. I only know that nothing is written in stone and we are not just replicas of our ancestors. We are our own being. We can make choices. We can change."

She paused and looked his way, though she could not see him. "I'll only say one thing more, about your father. You cannot trust him. Everything he says will be a lie. I saw that many times in the crystal. What you are confronting when you face him is a chameleon, someone who will shift and alter as he needs to in order to win, who will tell you what you want to hear, only to get the better of you so that he can destroy you. He will do anything to kill you, anything.

"I don't know what will happen—I can never see actual outcomes, just the process along the way. I only know that my fate is linked with yours. I don't know how to help you, but I want you to know that I want to help you. I *need* to help you. And if I can, I will, no matter what it costs me."

Still he said nothing and she turned away.

The van began the steady climb up a narrow mountain road, steep but curved around an enormous, jagged peak, climbing and climbing as if they were driving to heaven where, of course, neither of them would likely be admitted.

They ascended, her body pressed back against the seat. Unlike the vacillating weather in Germany, here, the temperature was icy. Suddenly she wondered if she would freeze to death from the chilly mountain air coming through the vent and overwhelming the vehicle's heater. She shoved the vent closed. She had the sleeping bag, but it was in the back.

She knew it was a good thing she couldn't see out the window and over the side of this slick road to the sheer drop hundreds of metres below; she would be screaming in terror.

When they ascended higher than she thought possible and she felt pressure in her ears and sinuses, suddenly they began to descend. At one point her ears popped and her nasal passages cleared. This night was devoted to rising and falling with the peaks that seemed endless, a long roller coaster ride through darkness, her stomach in knots. By the light of the nearly full moon, she could see from her peripheral vision what she thought was snow coming down, adding to the accumulation already on the ground. *We could be stranded here!* she thought, and that made her nervous, but she knew that idea was a diversion to keep from thinking about the vehicle plunging over a cliff.

She turned to Vlad, though even with moonlight she could only see a vague image and no details. He drove well and even in his current mental state was a competent driver. Vlad never tired of the drive. He seemed to be in a trance and she began to worry that the outcome of all this would not be a good one for him, or for her. He was about to face a powerful, ancient entity, that much she knew—her grandmother had told her this. A monster with no recognizable moral code. Not easily defeated by his youngest son, the sensitive son, the one who did not like to kill.

Finally they reached a valley and he pulled off the ice-covered road and drove over snow through a grove of trees. He got out and she followed. He lifted her into the back of the van and joined her in this casket he called a bed.

"Wait!" she said, before he could close the lid. "I need my sleeping bag or I'll freeze to death."

She crawled through the back of the vehicle, feeling around until her hand touched her suitcase. She undid the bungee cord and retrieved the bag.

As Lorelei climbed back into the *coffin* as she thought of the space where they slept and into the sleeping bag, zipping it up, she thought about the outside temperature; it was probably below freezing. The heater wasn't on because the ignition was off and she wondered how long it would take for the chassis to reach the same degree as the outside. She also wondered if she would survive twelve hours without heat in a thin sleeping bag meant for temperatures above zero.

As if he had read her mind, Vlad pulled her to him in the darkness and wrapped his body around her encased one. It was their first physical contact since the night he had killed his brother. He didn't try to penetrate her in any way and that, alone, worried her because it was not like him to not at least try. Had his will been sapped by the trauma of fratricide? Anyone's will would take a battering by such an act, even a vampire.

His flesh would cool over the light hours, she knew that. But maybe it would stay warmer than the temperature, at least enough to offer her some protection. *Protection*, she thought. *I could use some of that.*

Lorelei awoke the following sunset shivering but alive. She hadn't frozen to death. *Of course not!* she thought. *Fate isn't done with me yet.*

She relieved herself and ate some snow for moisture, but there was no food—everything extra she had bought was gone—and she knew there wouldn't be any for a while. Still, she had some water left, and filled the two empty large bottles with snow that would melt. She would be okay. She hoped.

He turned on the heater and the warmth brightened her mood, taking the chill from her bones, defrosting her.

She pulled out the crystal and right away saw three connecting lines. Bucharest, Brașov and Poenari, locations the audiobook had described and connected in her research of *Vlad Țepeș*. The first was the city where he had been imprisoned for ten years in a castle he built there. The second, the medieval town in which he met and fell for a Saxon princess. The third was a mountain top castle where he held back the Ottoman invaders, Poenari Castle in the Carpathian Mountains, where they were headed, far from civilization. All important places in the life of Vlad's ancestor.

The vehicle climbed yet another mountain, ascending the curved narrow road and she sensed that they had just about reached their destination.

She wanted to say something encouraging but she didn't know what that would be. After a struggle of selecting and discarding words and phrases, she settled for reaching over and gently touching his arm. Tonight, he did not brush her off, but he didn't acknowledge her either.

The moon was full and that light gave her a less hazy view of the world from the fragmented vision at the rims of her eyes. More mountains with snowy peaks. And in the distance what looked like distressed ruins of a medieval castle chiseled from the stone cliffs.

As they neared, the van picked up speed as if Vlad was in a hurry to get home. That unnerved her, but so much did now. There was no way to know the outcome and she did not feel strongly that it would either go well or badly. In fact, she felt torn, severed in two with worry and doubt and fear, all of it based on Vlad's apparently fragile mental state.

They reached what might have been a drawbridge—she heard the tires on what sounded like wood—and stopped. He got out and she did also, following him over the snow-covered wooden bridge that might have once spanned a moat, and onto a short, slippery, stone walkway.

She had read about this ravaged medieval castle, carved from the rock of a mountain peak, isolated and impenetrable. She heard creaking hinges, as if a rarely used door was opening inward.

It was cold outside but also cold inside. Her soles

slapped against flooring that was not wood, maybe smooth rock like slate.

Vlad moved quickly and she heard his boots ascend on what might be marble steps. She knew she'd reached the stairs because she fell forward when the toe of her sandal hit the front of the bottom step. She used her feet to feel along the front until she got to one end of the staircase. Reaching out, she groped until her hand hit a stone newel which led to a cold stone railing that she held tightly as she climbed.

The stairs were steep, each step worn and uneven, and it seemed to take forever to reach the top. Along the way a peculiar odor assaulted her nostrils and made her sneeze, one she could only categorize as ancient dust.

At the top landing she did not know which way to go.

"Ah, so it is you!" a voice cold as the grave said in English, clearly aware that she was there, wanting her to understand, and Lorelei walked that way, to her right.

"I have brought you gifts, Father," Vlad said.

She heard something heavy drop onto the floor and roll slightly, then something else much lighter in weight.

"The head of your brother. The bone of mine. Our family grows small. You and I are the same, now. Alone. Lonely." This was said in a tone that conveyed anything but loneliness.

He's smooth, she thought. *Too smooth*. Vlad's father had many centuries behind him that had sculpted and shaped and sanded his words to disguise his real intentions.

"Bring your brother here, my son," the father said, and

there was rustling, as if Vlad had picked up what he had dropped at the feet of his sire and then walked across the room.

Metal snapped like a lock opening, wood groaned, icy mountain air blasted through the already-cold room. "Give him to me!" the father demanded.

Vlad must have handed the head over and Lorelei had the sense that after a brief pause, it was tossed out a window to the cliffs below. The window slammed shut, the chilling breeze cut off.

"He was weak!" the old one said dismissively, his voice laced with detestation. But Lorelei heard an undercurrent —the son most like him, the one he liked most, was not in this room. "You are my only offspring now, and I have no wish to harm you," came the crafty voice. "We have no need for battle, my favorite son. I am old. Decrepit. You will one day take my place. I will soon give up my throne to you, my strongest offspring." Lorelei heard, and she wondered if Vlad did, that this was a complete lie. He had no intention of giving up anything.

Suddenly the old one said as though he hadn't seen Lorelei before this moment, but of course that could not be, since he did not speak in Romanian, "Another gift!"

A warning raced up her spine and her instinct was to turn and run for her life.

"My thoughtful son, you have no doubt brought her for me, and yet did not offer her with the others," the father chided. "An appeasement. To honor me, your sire, your lord, your master, whom you must obey." He paused again. "She is nothing, only food, but I will breed her and feed from her until she grows tiresome. Perhaps one day soon I will give her to you, but for now I will replenish myself and our line."

"She belongs to me," Vlad said, and Lorelei felt him moving close to her.

"Does she? I see no true marks." The smooth, reasonable voice grew louder as the old one seemed to glide towards them, a viper about to strike.

He sniffed the air deeply very close to her and she jolted. "She is virgin, untouched. You would have taken her if you wanted her, and you did not, so how can she belong to you? I take her as is my right; all that belongs to you belongs to me. She cannot be yours, but she will be mine."

A hand, skeletal, stroked her face and Lorelei cried out.

"No!" Vlad said, gripping her other arm, pulling her toward him.

By this action alone, Lorelei knew he could not win against this shrewd old vampire who had caused what must be tens if not hundreds of thousands of deaths and had brutalized as many or more. Vlad was not strong enough or wise enough. His distrust did not cut to the depth that would make him as wary as he needed to be. She felt her heart sink, hope blanketed by despair; her fate had been sealed and she sobbed once in the face of it.

She turned to Vlad. Unable to see him, she knew he could see her very well. "Let me go to him, please," she begged, trying to move her lips into a small smile that would belie her repugnance of the old one, hoping to hide the terror she knew must be reflected in her eyes. "It's my destiny." Despite her efforts at disguise, another sob slipped out of her mouth. She stared at his face, trying to see him, trying to tell him with her blinded eyes what words could not convey—if he did not release her willingly, the old one would kill him and take her anyway. If he let her go, Vlad might live—for a time, at least. Maybe enough time.

The father sounded matter-of-fact when he said, "To tame a *vrajitoarea* requires some skill. I have tamed many. I will teach you how, my youngest son.

"Come, *curvā*!" His voice turned hard. "You will soon learn your destiny is in *my* hands!"

She trembled uncontrollably as the boney fingers tore her away from Vlad, who did not intervene.

The old one began to remove the leather bag from her body and she held tight until he struck her across the face. She staggered backwards and her ears rang. He lifted the bag over her head and she heard him searching it.

"A sorceress's ball!" he laughed. "Is this how you defeated your brother?" the father asked Vlad, yet another stab at his confidence.

"Vlad was stronger!" Lorelei said, and the old vampire knocked her to the floor with his fist.

"*Curvā*! How dare you speak! I am *vampir*. You are less than the dust beneath my feet. You are nothing, *vrajitoarea*. Nothing! You live only to serve me!"

She heard the casement open again and then a far away sound of something glass-like shattering. Her heart skipped beats as she realized he had thrown her grandmother's crystal out the window where it broke into what must have been many pieces on the jagged rocks below. Her link to her grandmother was gone!

Lorelei sobbed loudly and buried her face in her hands. She heard the old one say, "You understand now, my son, this is what the *vrajitoarele* respect, and nothing less. Learn as I crush her will. Learn, my son, you who are the strongest."

The last word was said with such venom that Lorelei could not believe Vlad didn't hear this and react. But apparently he did not. She sensed him standing in the place where she had left him, paralyzed in the face of this omnipotent, brutal Lord of the Undead from whose sperm he had been formed and under whose viciousness he had been guided.

Strong hands yanked her to her feet and shoved her back. Her wrists were quickly bound together in front of her and then lifted above her head via something he attached to the rope tying her. Suddenly she was being hoisted off the ground.

Instantly her arms ached, her body felt stretched to the limit. Only the toes of her sandals touched the floor and not enough to take the pressure off her arms or allow her any equilibrium. Where he struck her, her lip had split and seeped blood that she tasted. She knew he smelled it, they both did, and that the fragrance for them must be tantalizing. She also knew it was just a matter of time until her blood fed the old one. She only hoped he would kill her outright and not torture her, but she realized how futile such a hope was.

He ripped the dress from her body savagely. Something leathery slid along her skin, like the finger of a glove, but not as flexible, stroking her nipple but not in an erotic way, then moving down and down and between her legs, threatening to enter her. The voice turned away from her. "The whip never fails, Vlad. You will recall its lessons, the sharp bite, the bitter sting, the deep marks that imprinted on you your position in my realm. Look how obedient you have become, you, your uncle, your dead brothers. You have done my bidding, all four of you." He paused and his voice grew even colder as he turned his face back in her direction, leaning close, the stale, fetid breath of centuries assaulting her. "She will kneel at my feet as you did. As you will again."

Lorelei's body twisted and she couldn't gain enough stability to stop the spinning. Tears gushed from her eyes. She knew what was to come and could not physically or emotionally brace herself against the onslaught. He would whip her into submission and then take all that Vlad could not; he would bring her to her knees and make her wish she was dead. But he would not kill her; he was merciless.

"Mamó, cabhrú liom!" she whispered to her grandmother, suddenly remembering the last words her mother's mother had spoken to her—'Born in blood, die in blood, and blood in between.'

Hard leather tore into the flesh of her back, forcing a

scream from her lips. The knife-sharp whip cut deep. She screamed even louder when it slashed her again, the hide sinking deeper this time, the pain more intense.

Suddenly the old man was on her, his icy tongue flicking like a snake's over the lines of blood beads the whip had created across her back. "Your blood tastes good, *vrajitoarea*! I will drink from you often before I stake you in my garden!" His long-dead fingers slid down her back and found both openings between her legs.

Grandmother! *Mamó*! she cried in her mind. *Save me!*

Her useless eyes leaked tears as she looked to where she thought Vlad stood. *Why are you letting this happen to me? He's tricking you. He'll kill both of us!* But she could not speak.

A cry filled the air, one close to her ear, deafening her for a moment. It sounded like hundreds, thousands of people in a death wail, reverberating like bells of demise. Then a swish, and with the sound hot liquid sprayed over her face and her naked, bleeding body.

Horrible sounds: squishing, stabbing, cutting, hacking. She knew she was listening to a body being dismembered. Terrified, Lorelei's every breath became a scream.

The casement opened; something was tossed out the window to the rocks below. Sounds came out of her mouth she could not control, not words, just incoherent babbling, as he came towards her rapidly like a powerful gust of glacial wind.

Hands grasped her wrists and tore apart the rope binding her wrists. She fell to the floor on her hands and knees and he was on her in a second. Vlad had become a demon through patricide and now nothing would keep him from her.

His teeth found her neck, pierced the skin and clamped on as he drew out her blood. At the same time his penis broke through other virgin flesh. He took her like the king of beasts mating, and the pain of this dual piercing staggered her to the point where she was startled to silence.

He was frenzied, being more aggressive than he needed to be, because now she did not resist him, could not resist him, but he didn't seem to notice. His hot body pummeled hers as he pushed deep inside and she felt split in two, all the while aware that her vision was becoming crystal clear.

The night waned but in the hours left he took her repeatedly, and she was astonished that there were so many ways. Each time she felt filled with him, her insides rubbed raw as he stroked her, stoking embers until she caught fire, her throat burning from the sucking that forced blood out of her body and into his leaving her depleted and ecstatic at the same time.

Only near dawn, when his strength began to ebb, did he revert to something resembling a human being. He kissed her, his lips wet with her blood, his body slowly bringing hers to a place it had not been before, beyond the pain and soreness to a pleasure that startled her as she convulsed and cried out in release.

As the darkness gave way to the light, he pulled her like an animal would drag its prey to a black corner of the room and lay with his hand gripping the back of her neck.

They both fell into an exhausted sleep.

✟

Lorelei woke to brightness and could still see and knew she would see from now on. Sunlight from the window bathed most of the room, but not the corner where they slept.

Her body tingled. She felt heavy and light at the same time. Sensitized. Sore. Yearning. Alive.

She turned her head and her breath caught at the beauty of his face. She'd never seen him so clearly or so close for such long moments and had no idea! Black hair, brows, long inky lashes, cheeks sculpted like the statue of the angel she had seen in a museum before she lost her sight. He was gorgeous. Gentle and fierce at the same time. Refined, barbaric. He looked angry and at peace. Such beauty brought tears to her eyes, blurring his image for a moment.

Seeing him made her happy and sad. When had he become her world?

Gently she removed his hand from the back of her neck and sat up dizzy, her head reeling.

The room was a sea of blood and body parts, but no heads. The old one had been staked through the heart from the back with the arm bone of his deceased brother. His decayed torso lay in the middle of the room, the whip still clutched in his hand across the room. The severed head—and she could not imagine the strength that took—must have gone out the window, as she believed she'd heard. She glanced down at her body. Blood streaked the insides of her thighs and was smeared across her breasts, her arms and she knew her face and neck and back must also be coated. Vlad's body was painted with her blood and probably his father's, turning much of his pale flesh crimson.

"You're so beautiful," she said to him, but he was asleep, of course, the sleep of the *vampir*, the day rest of the undead; he could not hear her. She bent and kissed his lips, examining close up a face that she knew she could gaze at for the rest of her life, if not forever. "I wish," she said softly, "that just once, you had called me Lorelei. Lora."

Finally, she stood on wobbly legs, picked up the leather bag and then carefully made her way to the stairs. All along the wall going down were portraits of Vlad's ancestors— she knew they were because he resembled them. There were only males, severe, humorless, stern. No females.

She headed out into the crisp mountain air and hurried naked to the van. More snow had fallen and she used the cold wetness to wash with and found her last dress in the suitcase in the back, a midi A-line blood-red velvet—*how appropriate*, she thought—and the eighteen-hole Docs. The snow she'd scooped into the bottles less than twenty-four hours before had melted then re-frozen, but the vehicle's heater would defrost the contents again soon enough. She swallowed a few handfuls of snow to keep her going.

The keys were in the van, as she knew they would be—he often left them in the ignition, likely for a quick get-away.

She adjusted the seat, snapped on the seatbelt and

looked in the rearview mirror. And stopped, stunned by what she saw. She had not seen her own face since she was a child. Viewer felt the way the viewed looked: awed. Her father was right: she did not need makeup. Eyes jade green, intense and luminous, copper eyebrows and lashes, long, curly wild hair down her back, red enough to catch fire, semi-full lips turned up at the corners but the lower one split and slightly swollen where the old vampire had hit her, and another swelling with a purple bruise beside her left eye. She looked serious and playful at the same time but her eyes reflected back at her the depth of the horror of what she had been through. She had changed. She was no longer a child and losing her virginity was the least of it.

She liked what she saw and although the visage was new to her, it was somehow familiar and comforting. She wondered if she looked as her grandmother had when she was young. Lorelei spent moments touching her face, her hair. And then she tilted the mirror downward so she could see her neck.

The marks were large and painful looking, and tender to the touch. His teeth had been precise, though, despite his frenzy, and absently she reached into the leather bag for the antibiotic ointment.

She also took out the Tarot deck still wrapped in the velvet fabric. No, not as precise as the crystal, but still a tool. She scanned the cards—this was the first time she had seen them—but then a memory struck. She had seen these cards before, when her grandmother did a reading for her as a child. The reading that spelled out her fate. The pastel colors, the lovely scenes of another time. And the darker cards, depicting the violence that would occur. She turned the cards over, shuffled them, then selected one at random. The Six of Cups. Two children. A card of unconditional love that made her smile.

After she applied some of the ointment, she tore the fabric in half lengthwise, making a scarf she wrapped around her throat to hide what, in this country, would have obvious meaning for ordinary people.

Her body pulsed with pain and a strange longing she had not experienced before that she knew was for him. Lorelei felt caught in a bittersweet pocket. She might have come to love him. She feared she already did love him. But by killing his brother and father—what he had to do, what he could not *not* do—he unwittingly played out the tradition of his line. And that worried her to distrust; he could just as easily play it out with her as well. And more importantly, with the twins she had conceived last night, the boy and the girl. The babies her grandmother had foretold. The ones for whom she had endured all this and because of them, her sight had been restored.

She could not trust Vlad. Her heart ached, ready to shatter at the impending loneliness she saw stretching before her.

Instead of succumbing to the powerful emotion, she turned the van and drove along the slick road carefully. She had driven before, with her grandmother, sitting on her lap just two days before her gram died, two days before

Lorelei's eighth birthday. Her grandmother explained how to drive and let her steer, even though she couldn't reach the pedals and couldn't even *see* the pedals, just focused on the road ahead. But her grandmother had been a good teacher and they spent all day and part of the night in the car and Lorelei had learned and that knowledge remained with her. She just wished her grandmother could be with her again. She'd have to be a memory now because Lorelei could no longer summon her energy through the crystal.

Even driving this slowly, she would be hours ahead of him, and so far she hadn't been aware that he could turn into a bat and fly. But it would take her many long hours if not days to cross the Carpathian Mountains, a task she did not relish at all, one that already filled her with dread. But she would do it and she would survive for the new lives forming within her.

She was headed to Ireland, to the house her grandmother had built and lived in all her life until she died the same hour her granddaughter had gone blind. The house Lorelei had inherited, along with the ball and the cards and the rosary. It was a small cottage located on an island in the Atlantic Ocean. It was hard to get to; only her dad knew of it, and he would never betray her. She and the babies would be safe. *He* would *never* find her.

As she drove at a snail's pace, the beauty of this rugged land struck her: sun glinting off snowy mountain peaks, wild trees that might have survived the harsh climate for millennia. Above, a large black bird soared in a line as if accompanying the van. Possibly a raven, her grandmother's favorite bird.

Her stomach growled and she drank more snow water trying to temper this need for food until she could find some in Brașov.

Suddenly, she remembered the apple she had tossed into her bag...when? It must have been more than a week ago. She rummaged around in the bottom of the bag and her fingers came to rest on the still-firm fruit. She stared at the green apple in wonder, feeling like Eve, the first woman, about to eat the first fruit of the tree of knowledge of good and evil.

She bit into it and tart-sweet juice filled her mouth. This was the best apple she had ever tasted, perfect in every way but one—it wasn't enough food. She would have to find more food and soon—she was eating for three now.

Nearly eight years later, when the twins were seven and Lorelei had established a life for the three of them in her grandmother's house on the island in the Atlantic off the west coast of Ireland, an island so small and remote that there were only two other residents, an elderly couple on the side facing the mainland who lived in their little cottage by the water, she opened her door one evening to find Vlad standing outside.

Over time, she knew he would come one night, but not when. The Tarot cards only revealed the inevitable, and she had dreaded this moment.

They stared at one another in silence for many long seconds until he said, "Invite me to enter."

She could not speak, only shook her head no.

Without the blood smears and other than the fact that he was fully dressed, he looked exactly as he had the last time she'd seen him when she ran away from the vampire lair in Romania. That long journey from there to here had been far from easy, fraught with perils that she preferred not to dwell on, but none of what occurred had come close to the horror of what she had experienced before she left him.

He stood in the early evening twilight, outside her door, dressed in black, the classically beautiful face and perfect body of a man in his mid to late thirties, appearing human and a mere thirteen or so years older than her now, unable to enter without an invitation, which she refused to extend.

"What do you want?" she demanded.

"Invite me to enter," he said again.

And again, she shook her head and this time said, "No."

They continued to stare at one another, although she avoided direct eye contact. Her refusal made him angry, but she remembered that anything could make this undead royalty angry. She had children now and her priority was to protect them, not to appease him.

Suddenly, the bedroom door opened and her twins raced out, chasing one another, laughing and shrieking. Lorelei spun around in a panic and grabbed her son, but her daughter flew past on the other side, out the door, and right into the arms of Vlad, who had stooped to intercept her.

"No!" Lorelei cried. "NO! Come back!" she called to her daughter, but it was too late.

He stood up, holding the child captive. Her daughter squirmed, staring first at her mother's terror-filled face, which frightened the girl, then at Vlad, who stared back at her with a look the child seemed to find fascinating and Lorelei hoped he wasn't hypnotizing her. Back and forth. Back and forth. Meanwhile, her son said over and over, "Ma, who's that, who's that?"

Lorelei couldn't speak but finally her daughter answered for her, "He's Daddy! Don't you 'member? Mommy draws us pictures of him all the time."

Vlad glanced at Lorelei and she pleaded with her eyes, fighting back tears. She stretched out her free hand and said, "Please, give her to me. She's just a child. Don't hurt her. Please."

"Are you our papa?" her son asked, also squirming, trying to get out of his mother's grasp. Lorelei kept him from approaching Vlad by holding the back of his t-shirt in a tight grip and he kicked her leg a couple of times to get free, something he did when he was extremely frustrated. The boy didn't handle frustration well, but then, neither did her daughter, traits they had no doubt inherited from their father.

"Stay here with me!" she said to her son in the toughest tone she had ever used with him, but it didn't seem to have any effect. He tried to pull away and hit her with his hand

and was at the start of a tantrum.

"Invite me in!" Vlad demanded, and Lorelei felt she had no choice.

"If you give me my daughter, you can enter."

He nodded once, set the squirming girl to the ground and took a step into the room.

The boy still struggled and the girl raced up to her brother, trying to pull him away from their mother.

"Stop that!" Lorelei cried. "Both of you!" But her tone had no effect. They yelled and screamed like feral children and she had a hard time keeping hold as she tried to pull them towards the bedroom so she could get them inside to safety and close the door.

"These children need discipline," Vlad said.

Suddenly her fury was directed toward him and blasted out of her. "Discipline? Like you received? So they can turn out like you? If you touch one hair on the heads of my babies, ever, I will kill you!"

This new tone made the children stop fighting and stare at their mother who had only raised her voice to them twice, once being five minutes ago.

Lorelei's body trembled with rage and fear. She looked at them, crouched down, and then pulled both to her, hugging them, holding them tight, caressing their heads, tears threatening to brim over her eyes. She tried to soften her tone and control her voice when she said, "I want you both to visit Mae. She'll give you cookies and milk and you can play with Bunny. Tell Mae mommy has a visitor and you need to stay there tonight."

"I don't want to go!" the girl yelled. "I want to play with Daddy!"

"You said our daddy was dead!" her son accused.

My god, she thought. *All those pictures I've drawn for them over the years, all the fabricated stories I've told them about Vlad. They think he's an angel!*

"Daddy can't play with you now. Tomorrow you can play. Mommy and Daddy have to talk now. Go to Mae's and play there and in the morning, I'll come get you." *If I'm alive*, she thought.

More cajoling took place before they would agree to leave, and still she couldn't get them out. Finally, Vlad interjected, "Obey your mother!" in a voice that held a firmness that stopped their bad behavior instantly. The twins stared up at him, mouths gaping, eyes very round. He looked at Lorelei and said, "Discipline is not always brutal but it is important to contain children."

She shot him a fierce look. What the hell did he know about children? *She* had raised them, not him. Alone!

But his tone was as effective as hers had not been and finally she managed to get her little ones to leave, escorting them to the door past Vlad.

Her daughter asked Vlad on the way out, "Will you play games with us?"

Before he could answer, Lorelei did for him. "Not now. Hurry to Mae's before all the cookies are gone."

Gently but firmly she shoved them out the door then closed it, moving to the window to make sure they were leaving; she watched them running down the path as the sky darkened and night fell.

Once they were safe, she turned, only to find him too close. "What do you want?" she snapped.

"Why did you turn against me?"

She tried to walk past him but he grabbed her arm. She stared at his pale hand, his grip like iron, then looked up into his breathtaking face. "I didn't turn against you. I did what you wanted, led you to your brother. I went with you to your home. My job was done." She tried to make her face expressionless to emphasize that explanation but knew he wouldn't be satisfied with it, and he wasn't.

His eyes narrowed. "You belong to me." He said it as if he'd said a car belonged to him, or a pair of shoes.

Now it was her turn for anger. "No, I don't, King of the *Vampirii!* I was volunteer labor, free hired help, that's all. I did my job. You fucked me and drank my blood, a nice added perk with the servants when you rule the universe. It's over. Go!"

His dark eyes turned hard. "Why?"

"You're hurting me!" she said, nodding at her arm. "Maybe you don't care or maybe you want to hurt me, but I wish you'd stop."

He let her go.

She felt exhausted, perhaps from years of worrying about just this moment, when he would appear, when he would confront her on running away. When he would discover that he had two children.

Lorelei took a seat at the small table with three chairs, feeling tense and somehow defeated. He also sat, but next to her, not opposite. She didn't have the strength to care that he was so close.

They were both silent for quite a while until finally he said, "You have vision," a statement only, nothing hidden in it that she could discern.

"Yes. Every time you tried to penetrate me, anywhere, I could see a little, but only for seconds, it didn't last. And then, that final night, when you... Then, well, my eyes healed and I've been able to see since. The change is permanent."

He studied her face and she turned away from such intense scrutiny.

"Why did you leave?"

It was so complicated, she didn't know where to begin. She'd thought about this so often over the years and her feelings and reasons had gone from murky to clear and back to murky, constantly vacillating.

"Tell me before this no longer matters to me," he said, and she felt that statement might be ominous in some way.

"I had to protect my babies."

He looked confused.

"I knew you had impregnated me that night; I felt it. And my grandmother told me it would happen; it was my fate. That's why I had to help you. Because if it wasn't you, it would have been your brother or your uncle. Or your father." Her voice faltered when she mentioned his father. "And she said it should be you. And then it was you who won, but I knew I couldn't stay there, with you, because of the babies."

"I do not understand."

"Isn't it obvious?"

"It is not obvious to me."

"Vlad, you killed your brother. And your father and—"

"I had no choice! You know that. You were there!"

"I know what happened. But maybe there was another way—"

"There was no other way! It is tradition—"

"Which is why I had to leave."

"Explain!"

"How can you be so dense!" she snapped. His eyes narrowed. "I'm sorry. I'm stressed. But I don't know how you can't see what happened."

He waited.

"Yes, you followed tradition. And that's the problem. You killed them. You were victorious, with my help, I might add, and now you're king or emperor or pope, with whatever that entails. You followed tradition exactly. And you would have followed tradition with me, using me for blood and sex until you were bored, then killing me—"

"No!"

"—me, who would have been like your wife in a sense—"

"—you *are* my wife!"

That stopped her for a second. But she had to go on, say it all. "And you would have killed our daughter just because she's female."

"Why do you say such things?"

"And force your son to fight you to the death as your father forced you to fight him so that you won't be usurped. You would have killed us all. *That* is your tradition!"

"How can you believe this?"

She could only shake her head and swipe angrily at the tears leaking from her eyes.

He stood suddenly, looking perturbed, and the chair he had sat on teetered. He paced the small room, stalking, really, while she sat at the table watching him, feeling his unpredictability, fearful that he would turn on her any second like an enraged beast. If he killed her, who would take care of her little ones? Who would keep them safe from the *vampir*? After everything she had gone through, how had it come to this?

Suddenly he stopped by her chair and stared down at her. She felt intimidated and stood immediately, turning away from him, but he caught her arms, pulling her close, staring into her eyes, his unfathomable. "I am not my father!"

"I don't know that," she said, pushing his hands away, and he let her go.

She felt frightened, confused, inexplicably hopeless and hopeful at the same moment, so agitated that she now began pacing the small room herself. "Don't tell me you wouldn't drink my blood every chance you get!"

"I am capable of controlling my needs."

"How?" She stopped and stared at him. "Don't lie to me."

"I have never lied to you."

He paused, then said, "I control my urges already. I do

not require much blood. I told you this before. With you, it was more difficult, but I can learn to do this."

"I can't let you hurt my children."

"They are *my* children as well. I would not harm them."

"No, just beat them into submission."

He looked angry again. "Why do you think this of me? Have I beaten you?"

"You let your father whip me!"

"*Gresesti!*" he snapped, throwing up a hand, and then sighed heavily in frustration, squaring his shoulders defensively.

"I needed him to taste your blood, which I knew he could not resist, if only to humiliate me further. I needed him to believe I was weak, submissive to his will. He was powerful, strong, wily; he had lived many more centuries than me. I had one chance only, while the blood absorbed him. Otherwise, I could not have saved you. Or myself. Can you not see this?"

Confusion overwhelmed her. She had no idea he had thought all that out, had planned it. She remembered feeling at the time that he had let her walk right into the path of a fire-breathing dragon because he didn't care.

Suddenly, she felt drawn to him and suspected he was drawn to her, or at least to her blood. "Don't look me in the eye! You're casting a spell on me!"

He took two steps towards her and she backed up until she hit the wall. He lifted a hand and she flinched. "Do not be afraid," he said.

Gently, he touched her fiery hair, smoothing it back

from her face, behind her shoulders. He lifted her chin and leaned down to kiss her lips, slowly, softly. She wanted to resist, but the feel of this, so long missing in her life, left her sighing and her lips parted against her will as did his lips and his tongue entered her mouth. The kiss became warm and wet and passionate, full of movement, an erotic dance, leaving her breathless.

He stopped the kiss, his face very close to hers. "Your name is Lorelei. Lora. A siren from Germany who lures males as you have always lured me. It is you who has cast a spell, on me."

That stunned her and yet something in her knew it was true. He was here partially because she drew him, even as he drew her.

They kissed again, their lips more passionate, her body responding in a way she had forgotten was possible—it had been so long. But when he began to knead her breast, waking her skin after eight years of suppressed sensation, a physical memory resurrected and every cell opened to him as did her heart and soul.

Soon, his arm snaked her waist and he walked her backwards to the narrow bed where she slept in the corner of the room. He undressed her and she took off his clothes and then he pressed her down onto the bed and lay on top of her.

She felt him hard against her and that thrilled and terrified her, anticipating what would come. Every inch of her flesh was caressed by his lips or hands and she arched to meet him as a deep yearning overtook whatever logic she still possessed.

His skin felt cool but not cold and her fingers traced the strong defined muscles of his slender frame, making her want him more. She ran her hands through his hair, pulling his mouth to hers again, starving for this.

So much time apart acted as foreplay and she spread her legs and bent her knees and he entered her immediately, sliding deep into her moist darkness, making her gasp; she was so hungry!

They both came quickly and he stayed inside her, holding her around the waist, her arms around his neck, locking him to her, until desire grew again and he moved and she moaned and cried his name, this time releasing herself to him more fully along with a flood of tears.

His mouth found her neck, eye-teeth poised, and she sensed the tension in him as his body quivered, struggling for restraint.

"Control is probably best learned slowly," she said, moving her long red hair back, inviting the dark kiss.

He took her that way, piercing quickly and cleanly, holding her close and she could feel her blood flow into him as she listened to the sucking and lapping sounds. He drank only a little, for seconds, nothing near what he had taken that last night in Romania, which had left her so weak.

While he drank he lifted her a little, his ardor rekindled and she grabbed onto him, her hands like vices clamped to his shoulders, until he breathed her name into her ear and she cried out in a volcanic explosion of passion, her body quaking, shuddering, her mind emptied of fears and worries and expectations, finally handing over the part of her that already belonged to him.

⸙

As dawn approached, he removed her arms and said, "I must seek shelter from the light."

"Wait," she told him, rising from the bed. She knelt on the floor and lifted the part of the bed skirt that draped over the side, then pulled out a large box by two handles, the structure as long and wide as the bed beneath which it was stored.

"I built this for you," she said.

He sat up. "You knew I would come?"

"Yes."

"But you have no crystal! How could you know?"

"The cards. I can see them. I can't see other images but I feel those."

She opened the drawer of her bedside table and unwrapped the divination tool she'd had with her eight years ago, searching until she found the Ten of Cups and showing him the image of a mother, father and two children standing under a rainbow.

He looked awed, and somehow, that delighted her. He must have looked this way in the past, several times, but back then she couldn't see him. Now she could. And it confirmed to her what she had always known in the deepest part of herself: he wasn't his father. He was the sensitive one, the one expected to not survive. But survive he did. Because of her. And she knew it wasn't just that she had helped him locate the ones who wanted him dead. He had a stronger reason to survive; he fought for himself but also to save her.

She understood that even though he could not speak the word *love*, he felt it. It had only taken eight years for her name to come from his lips. She could wait to hear this word. She knew that one day, in the future, when the children had grown older, he would make her like him— her grandmother had told her that too.

"Sleep here," she said. "You'll be safe. I'll protect you. Always. And tomorrow night, you can get to know your children. Our children. They're so very much like you. And me."

The End ✟ *Sfarsit* ✟ *An deireadh* ✟ *Das End*

Dear Reader, Thank You!

I am so grateful that you have read my little novella. Reviews help authors tremendously, so do feel free to review this book.

If you enjoyed *Wild Hunt*, please check out my **Thrones of Blood** vampire novel series, available in both eBook and print.

> *Vol 1 - Revenge of the Vampir King*
> *(read an excerpt below)*
>
> *Vol 2 - Sacrifice of the Hybrid Princess*
>
> *Vol 3 - Abduction of Two Rulers*
>
> *Vol 4 - Savagery of the Rebel King*
>
> *Vol 5 - Anguish of the Sapiens Queen*
>
> *Vol 6 - Imperilment of the Hybrids*
> *(in 2020)*

May the best of the dark and mysterious world be with you!

Nancy Kilpatrick

THRONES OF BLOOD

Volume 1 - Revenge of the Vampir King

Chapter One

Moarte sat impatiently on the black marble throne watching the parade of his warriors as they entered the cavernous grey-stone throne room in sixes through the massive Oak doors. Directing this procession was Wolfsbane, his second-in-command. His most trusted warrior dressed like all the other tall and lean vampirii streaming in: sleeveless black metallic banded shirt and kilt, knee-high black leather boots laced through forty holes—battle gear. The vampirii style favored long hair pulled severely back on the head through a metal cone that contrasted in color to the hair, the strands dangling down the back like the tail of a horse. Even after nearly two hundred years as King of the vampirii, Moarte still felt a welling of pride as he watched this assembly of his strongest and bravest.

On display was booty garnered from their raid on the Sapiens realm. There were ruby red, sapphire blue and aventurine green jewels of varying shapes and sizes, hammered copper and gold bracelets, luxurious black and white furs, multi-hued cloth woven to a fine, soft texture, delicate hardwood furniture inlaid with ivory and ebony, aromatic spices used by the slaves for cooking, small animals of every sort kept as pets... It went on and on, most useless items in Moarte's view, for what did his realm of Deathbringers need with such goods. His warriors, all of his subjects but for the slaves, they were *vampirii*, living on blood, and these items might be interesting entertainment now and again, but were completely unnecessary to existence. And secretly he thought luxuries encouraged weakness in those of his kind. Whether birthed as he had been or turned as every other *vampir* in his realm, all were innately hunters, predators, and their skills relied on honing hungers to motivate them, not the acquisition of looted objects. But there were many types of hunger and blood was but one of them. Revenge was another, and Moarte was filled with that, a lust he had begun to acquire half a year ago and that appetite had become an all-pervasive driving force.

"The land of the Sapiens is rich with goods," Wolfsbane noted. He was a handsome *vampir*, with wavy dark brown hair and penetrating eyes the color of jade. Strong. Powerful. And Moarte relied on him.

"We swarmed and ravaged the mortals as revenge for what they did to you, our King," Wolfsbane continued. "These are your prizes which we offer to you in adoration."

Moarte nodded, uncomfortable that his troops had been gone almost half a moon's cycle without him leading them. But he had been in no shape to return to the realm of the Sapiens after the physical, mental and emotional torture his enemies had inflicted on him. His body had recovered sufficiently and nearly so his mind, but he did not feel whole. A passion for vengeance sliced through him at the oddest moments, and he knew he had been changed forever by what he had endured as a prisoner.

He felt required to accept the spoils of war from his faithful as an indirect revenge, but it rankled. He would have preferred to be in the forefront of battle, rending and tearing his enemy limb from limb, the Sapiens ruler at the top of his list.

The row upon row of items brought into his throne room were symbolic, he knew, which is why he let this lavish show proceed. His subjects needed to affirm in his presence that they had been victorious against the mortals and they needed to see that their efforts pleased him. But *he* needed something more, and hoped this glut of goods would culminate in the knowledge he craved: that Wolfsbane had either secured the Sapiens King and brought him to the land of the *vampirii*, or had killed him. Moarte would have preferred the former, of course—revenge is sweetest when executed directly— but he would settle for the demise of his enemy at the hand of another. Bringing down the Sapiens King from the far side of the mountains would insure peace and stability and danger-free hunting, at least for a time, and he wanted that for his Kingdom. He owed it to his subjects.

Incense, flora, leather, some exotic blue and green birds that he had never seen... It was an endless parade, including captive Sapiens by the dozen, male and female, all young enough to be pleasing to look at, but he knew that most of his followers were not examining their faces and bodies but rather smelling the blood coursing beneath skin slick with acidic sweat produced by terror.

"I selected only the strongest, my lord, as I knew you would prefer. You have often said: *There is no point in taking the weak. Their blood is thin and prone to disease and that does not satisfy.*"

"I've said many things, my most trusted warrior, and you have a good memory," Moarte said, his features unable, like all *vampirii*, to reflect the smile he felt. "If I had not known you for centuries, I would accuse you of flattering me unduly with some hidden agenda."

"I am not my sister!" Wolfsbane said with a touch of annoyance in his voice, referring to Hemlock, his twin, who on more than one occasion had tried to charm Moarte in order to be granted power. Hemlock would have liked nothing better than to be chosen by Moarte as his mate. Fortunately, as King by birth and not by transformation, Moarte had inherited a type of rational second sight from his blonde haired, blue-eyed mother Belladonna, and a searing intellect and physical strength from his late father, Morpheus, who had platinum hair and paler eyes. They bestowed fortitude and attractiveness as well and Moarte, even had he not been King, would have had his pick of females. Hemlock had not gotten far with such duplicitous endeavours. When he mated, *if* he ever mated—and with the passing of time, that seemed improbable to him—it would be with a guileless female; he possessed enough guile in his character for two beings.

"And where is Hemlock?" Moarte inquired, realizing he had not seen her in some time and she was not in the throng of warriors crowding the hall. "Did she venture on the hunt with you?"

"No, she did not. Her battle skills are not lacking but I felt we did not require her presence in this campaign. I suspect she has retreated to her chamber in a prolonged pout."

Moarte felt some amusement at this. It was well known that Wolfsbane and Hemlock were adversaries in many ways and that given his position as second in command of *vampir* warriors, Wolfsbane frequently deprived his sister of positions she would otherwise have automatically assumed. Partly this was out of spite, Moarte knew, but also out of expediency. Hemlock was unpredictable and not given to following orders, traits that were dangerous in battle.

Larger animals were brought into the hall, their strong odor annoying to the olfactory of *vampirii*, and Moarte said tensely, "Wolfsbane, when may I expect this exhibition to end? I have more pressing matters to attend to than watching my subjects entertain themselves with these treasures."

"Calmness, my son," Belladonna, seated to his right, said. "Your warriors need to see your enthusiasm. It's part of the vanquishing of a long-time enemy."

"I have not vanquished him yet, Mother, unless Wolfsbane knows more than he is saying about the raid. Is the Sapiens King part of this circus?"

The question was directed to Wolfsbane, who answered truthfully, as always, because he knew Moarte could read him very well and there was no use in avoidance. "No, my King, he is not."

"Then you did not find him in the city."

Wolfsbane hesitated. "We did find him."

"And?"

"He managed to elude us. He distracted us and must have escaped through a secret passageway into the mountain's caves."

Moarte felt the small amount of blood in his veins heat to boiling. They had lost him! The one who had tortured Moarte for weeks. The entire raid was a waste! He *knew* he should have led the hunt! He should not have remained behind, broken though he was. If he had gone, or denied the request and waited until he was strong again, the Sapiens King would not have evaded his fate. The breather's blood would now be swelling Moarte's veins, his head staked and hanging from the highest tower, a trophy of war, a final victory over the persecutors of the *vampirii*. His soul would be—

"But King Moarte, I have brought you something almost as good."

Moarte wondered what that could be, since nothing would equate with the capture of the Sapiens King. He waited. And then his eyes fell upon the last item that was being brought into the throne room, a large cage covered by purple velvet, carried on horizontal poles on the shoulders of four of his sturdiest bloodsuckers.

"What is this? Another animal?" he snapped impatiently, his tone a warning that everyone in the room understood and, because of the danger inherent in their King's temper, fell silent.

"This is a gift to you from the Sapiens King. One he offered as a token of his desire for peace. It was during this exchange that he vanished, which I deeply regret. My King, it was my fault entirely and I throw myself on your mercy now."

Wolfsbane knelt before Moarte, head back, exposing his throat for the fangs.

Aggravated, Moarte ordered, "Stand!" and waved a hand dismissively, indicating that he had no intention of punishing Wolfsbane. Wolfsbane was an excellent warrior, a friend even, one of the few Moarte trusted implicitly. And in a way he was glad the Sapiens King had escaped; it meant he still lived and that would allow Moarte to hunt down his enemy himself, and that thought gave him no small amount of pleasure.

The warriors parted to let the bearers bring the cage— tall enough to house a newborn giraffe—almost to the bottom of the three grey-marble steps that led to the throne. At Wolfsbane's order, they lowered it onto the slate floor.

"You say this is an offering?" Belladonna asked. As the former Queen of the realm, she held a place of honor by Moarte's side. Upon the death of her husband Morpheus, Moarte's father, she assumed the reign, but only for a short time before relinquishing her right to rule, clearing the throne for her son, the only known half-breed, born when she was still Sapiens. At times, though, she did not remember that she no longer held real power.

"Yes, Dowager," Wolfsbane said. "The Sapiens King offered this to effect a truce. We did, of course, not agree to a truce, but as I mentioned, the offer left us startled and confused and this afforded the Sapiens ruler a means of escape, which we now see as having been planned."

"Indeed. A rather poor excuse for your error in judgment. Or was it simply incompetence?" Belladonna said.

Wolfsbane bowed in her direction. If she were still in charge and he bared his neck, her teeth would have been in his jugular by now, and he knew it.

Moarte said, "Mistakes occur, Mother. I have made them myself, as you well know. As have you."

She nodded slightly and surreptitiously brushed her son's bare arm to validate his remark, careful not to let the *vampirii* see this intimate motherly act.

Moarte did not acknowledge this touch of flesh as cold as his own. Instead, he said, "Alright, Wolfsbane, you have whetted my curiosity, and I wish to see an end to this pageantry. What is this wondrous gift the Sapiens King sent my way to make up for a month of torture in his dungeon?"

Wolfsbane inclined his head slightly towards Moarte and then walked to the cage. Quickly he pulled back the purple fabric and as it lifted, wooden bars were revealed, like a prison holding something feral. What came into view *was* feral. The silence in the cavernous hall echoed like a piercing shriek.

Moarte stared, struck dumb, unable to believe what he was seeing.

"My lord, the Sapiens King offered you his daughter in marriage, to save his Kingdom, to bind our realm to his, but really to save himself."

"Liar!" the black-haired mortal screamed through the bars where her wrists were bound on either side of her. "My father would *never* agree to such a deal. You're despicable, all of you vile, dead things!" Her slim, tense body was clothed from the top of her neck to her ankles in a crimson dress of silk. Her dark eyes shot a fiery malevolence towards Wolfsbane, and her teeth gnashed together twice as if she would bite through the wooden doweling and disembowel him. But Wolfsbane was not watching her. He, like everyone else in the room, was watching Moarte.

Moarte rose dangerously slowly, like the predator he knew himself to be. A predator fixated on prey. His mother attempted to secretly touch his arm again, to temper him, but he ignored her. His eyes were glued to the girl, the Sapiens Princess Valada, only child of the Sapiens King. Despite what the Sapiens King had ordered done to him, *she* was the one who had tried to maim him which, ironically, had provided him with the intense motivation necessary to find a means to escape that realm and make his way home. It took nearly a full moon's cycle to walk over the high mountain because he could not fly and his body was so damaged. There was almost no food but for the blood of the small earth-bound creatures he could catch; starvation kept him from recovering. He finally reached the *vampirii* stronghold barely alive, a state that required many more months from which to recover.

And now, before him, was one of his two tormentors; it was a dream come true.

His movement had brought the girl's attention his way. He remembered her clearly, very clearly, and knew she remembered him—how could she not? It had been her hand that snapped the fine bones in his wings so that he could not escape through flight. Despite the *vampirii* ability to heal rapidly, some injuries were fatal and others nearly so and took much time to heal, if ever they did fully heal. The broken wing bones had required nearly one month to knit themselves together, partially because of his enfeebled state and partially because they had melded wrong and, when he reached home, had to be rebroken, only adding to the excruciating pain. His mother's ministrations with the salves and drugs made of herbs she had learned to recognize as a girl when she was still mortal helped. But much of the healing time involved him lying in agony, drinking as much vitae as he could keep down, building his strength back one night at a time by sheer will, as the bones slowly wove together properly. And all the while he nurtured a white-hot hatred for this girl as the scalding desire for revenge festering within him. It was Wolfsbane who could not bear his suffering and insisted that Moarte allow the warriors to attack the Sapiens city and hunt down their King.

Moarte moved slowly down the three steps, never taking

his eyes off her. She was proud and haughty still, not accepting that she was a prisoner, and one given freely to him by her treacherous father.

"Bloodsucker!" she snarled as he neared the cage, her dark eyes flashing hatred and defiance, and she spit at him. He paced slowly in front of her in one direction, then the other, many times, back and forth, silent, his fangs extended, his eyes which he knew had turned the color of blood, radiating fury, never leaving her face, her eyes following him, the tension palatable to all in the throne room.

"I should have torn them off!" the girl shrieked loudly in the quiet hall, referring to his wings.

He stopped before her and stared down at the Sapiens Princess with hair and eyes the color of a raven's feathers and skin nearly as pale as his own. The bloody-red dress, the black hair and eyes, all of it made for a startling contrast with her calcimine flesh and she looked like a corpse to him, one more than twenty but not yet thirty of the Sapiens years. It was rumored by the slaves that she was truly her father's daughter, his only offspring, who he may or may not have been grooming to inherit his throne. Rumor also had it that his new young wife had conceived with the hope of a boy, but may have died in childbirth, the life in her womb dying with her. Wolfsbane would unearth the facts in detail from the newest Sapiens slaves he had brought back with him.

It was said this girl Valada was a virgin still, refusing to marry, and only in that regard going against her father's wishes; the father no doubt wanted a grandson to hand his crown to, since the Sapiens preferred male rulers. It was known that otherwise she was devoted to him, wholeheartedly so, even when his subjects were not so enamored of their treacherous, brutal ruler.

But her blindness to the reality of the Sapiens King's cruelty did not alter Moarte's feelings towards her. His rage was so close to erupting that he felt on the verge of cracking the bars and snapping her head off her shoulders, gorging on her blood. He had enough control at his disposal to realize that such an action would give him immense pleasure, but only momentarily. The calculating reason that his father bequeathed him kicked in; if he was smart, he would use her in a way that would lead him directly to the Sapiens King. And then he could destroy both father and daughter at the same time.

His voice hummed perilously low, the result of holding himself in check. "Take the cage to my chamber!"

Wolfsbane gestured and the four warriors lifted the cage. As they removed her from his sight, he watched her and she watched him, holding one another's hostile gaze until the cage rounded a corner and was gone.

Moarte was excited, rattled, brimming with violence and anger, logic in shockingly short supply. He would need time to summon thought to aid him. This was a rare opportunity. He had at hand one of his two enemies, the one he had spent months dreaming about, his fantasies of exacting revenge for her cruel and callous act towards him delicious and all-consuming. And she had been delivered into his hands by her own father! This was a precious gift that he must use carefully. Yes, it required much thought.

"You did well, Wolfsbane," he said, his voice still low, betraying the control he fought hard to retain.

As if coming out of a trance he woke to the hall and knew that direction was expected of him. "Secure one quarter of the riches for the crown, and half that again for yourself. The rest is to be divided between the warriors, starting with these," he said, his hand sweeping across the front line, indicating the males and females who were the oldest and strongest, his premier warriors who made up the bulk of his war council and had proven their bravery and loyalty time and time again. "They will choose first, then the rest."

Wolfsbane knelt, as did the first line of warriors, and behind them the others fell to their knees as one body, throats exposed before their ruler as a sign of deference.

Moarte stalked out of the throne room through the side exit, the heat within him rising again to match the emotional fury he could no longer keep at bay. He needed time in solitude and headed for the locked gardens behind the castle, his private world where none, not even his mother, were permitted to enter; he would meditate on this 'gift' and what he could do with it and he would not be disturbed as he entertained strategies. But the thinking part of him was nearly obliterated by emotions and if the Sapiens King had been killed in the raid, Moarte knew he would have torn the girl limb from limb quickly, publically, glutting himself on her blood, just for the sheer pleasure of it. And that image brought a smile to his lips. He could always do that once her father had been killed. And would.

Chapter Two

Valada, encaged, had been transported to the private chamber of the King of the vampirii and there she waited, knowing that whatever he did to her, it would be brutal. The bloodsuckers were cruel, violent, and liars—her father had proclaimed that often enough, and every Sapiens knew it. If these undead things thought they could somehow wear her down by saying her father handed her over to them like some prize so that he could escape... No, that was something she would never believe! Her sire was a good ruler, a fair man, one who needed her help to control a Kingdom of rebels; the throne had been his destiny and, by inheritance, would be hers. The bloodsuckers were just trying to torment her...before the real torture began.

Moarte would show her no mercy. She could see that in his red eyes, the hatred for clipping his wings. He would take revenge on her because her father was not available for revenge. She had to steel herself for whatever he threw at her until her father could reform his army and rescue her from these night creatures that only wanted the blood of the living like her to fill their veins. She was a prisoner, at the mercy of beings who were merciless. Creatures that had preyed upon Sapiens since the beginning of time.

Undead, inhuman, cold, soulless entities that should not exist, and yet they did. The nightmare of the living.

She was strong and would have to remain strong, but she felt both exhausted and agitated. Partly, it was the fear generated by imagining what horrors would come her way. Partly it was what she had already undergone. She had been bound for a full day as they traveled over the mountain and into the land of the *vampirii* with slaves and animals and goods, then tied in this way inside this cage for the last hour of the long journey. Her arms throbbed, her hands were red and numb from the ropes tight around her wrists, her legs ached and she knew if the rough hemp wasn't holding her up she would collapse. Added to that and the lack of sleep, they had not fed her for at least twenty-four hours and she had only received enough water throughout the trip to keep her alive—the one called Wolfsbane told her that. He also said, "King Moarte will be happy to have you, and all the better if you are in good enough shape for his purposes. Prepare yourself for the worst!"

There were no windows in this large and desolate room made of grey stone, only a vast open space with little furniture, a walk-in fireplace, and not much more. The stone room opened onto a stone balcony with a three foot ledge surrounding it. She could tell from the trees in the distance that she was high up in this fortress but not in a tower. High enough that perhaps she could not escape but she might be able to fling herself over the balcony and die from the fall if it came to that. Anything but to be in the hands of this monster who had killed her mother.

All her life Valada had wanted revenge for her mother's murder and her father had assured everyone that one day it would happen. One day the King of the *Vampirii* would be in their hands. And her father had been right! She'd had an opportunity to avenge her mother. The bloodsucker King was snared in a mesh trap made of metal when he flew over the border between their lands and above their castle. The minute she knew he had been captured, she raced down to the dungeon where her father kept him, just to see for herself this demon that had drained her mother's blood. And thanks to her quick thinking, she had a guard bring her pruning shears and snapped the bones of his wings with her own hands so that he could not escape by flight. She had been so excited by the act that she could not speak. The securely bound *vampir* King had not uttered one sound but had glared at her with hatred and she snapped as many bones as she could and laughed in his face, feeling insane.

She could not understand why her father had not destroyed the bloodsucker outright; had she been ruler of the Sapiens she would have. Even the pleasure of torture would have been relinquished just to watch him writhe and burn in the sunlight where she would have chained him. He and he alone was responsible for her mother's death. And she knew that because her father had witnessed it with his own eyes, helpless to aid her mother, and had often told the story when he held court:

One night, when Valada was three years old, the creature had swooped in, gliding through the air on those same enormous black wings, like a giant bat, right into their rooms. Her father had fought him, of course, but had been asleep, taken by surprise, no match for the superhuman strength of the undead. He was knocked to the ground, hit his head, and only awoke in time to see the bloodsucker tear into the flesh of her mother and steal all the blood from her veins, leaving just an empty shell.

Valada had apparently been in the room with them, but she was so young she remembered nothing. No, that wasn't true. She remembered the stench of blood. An overwhelming odor that had filled her with horror and to this day she could not bear the rank smell.

And now she would choke on the smell of blood again, when the *vampir* King took hers. She only hoped he would be quick about it because she had no idea how long her father would be in rescuing her. And if she was completely honest with herself, Valada realized that forming an army of what soldiers has been left alive and intact in the city would be difficult and time-consuming and realistically she could not expect rescue soon.

And likely not soon enough. She would probably not be alive long, ravaged by this slayer of the Sapiens. She vowed to find a way to antagonize him so that he would lose control and kill her quickly, putting her out of the misery she knew would come. Above all, she wanted to die proudly, the daughter of a proud ruler, bringing glory to his name and to the Sapiens. She refused to die a victim.

But her mind kept returning to one thing: how had he escaped, this undead King of the *vampirii*? He had been under their control, securely chained to a wall and locked in the dungeon cell. It was inconceivable. He must have had help, but who—

Amidst these thoughts he entered the chamber, his pale eyes fixed on her dark eyes. She felt like prey. How else could she feel; he was a predator.

To continue this story, pick up a copy of *Revenge of the Vampir King* at your favorite online or brick-and-mortar bookstore.

About the Author

Nancy Kilpatrick is an award-winning author who has published 23 novels, over 220 short stories, and 7 collections of her stories, and has edited 15 anthologies, plus scripted graphic novels and written and compiled the non-fiction book *The goth Bible: A Compendium for the Darkly Inclined* (St. Martin's Press). *Thrones of Blood,* Vols 1 to 6 (Crossroad Press), her newest series of non-sparkling vampire novels for adults, is currently in the process of being optioned for television.

Nancy lives in lovely Montréal and enjoys travelling the world—aka the Great Curio Cabinet—ferreting out oddities of people, places and things. If you'd like to get in touch, connect with her here:

Facebook: nancykilpatrick.31
Twitter: @nancykwriter
Blog: nancykilpatrickwriter.blogspot.com
Instagram: nancykilpatrickauthor
Newsletter: Once a month & brief. Sign up at my website.
Website: nancykilpatrick.com

Coming soon from Baskerville Books:

Do You Know Me?

a collection of
short stoies
by

Caro Soles

Baskerville Books

CPSIA information can be obtained
at www.ICGtesting.com
Printed in the USA
LVHW050730240423
744513LV00002BA/13